FATAL FOOTNOTE

A LIBRARY COZY MYSTERY OF MURDER, MAYHEM, AND MANUSCRIPTS

MAPLEWOOD MYSTERIES
BOOK 2

KATHLEEN GUIRE

CHAPTER 1

THE GREAT LITERARY EGO PARADE

MY SANITY HAD ALREADY GONE DOWN the drain, and the official author reading hadn't even started yet.

"You call this tea hot? It is tepid, that is what it is," Veronica Steele, celebrity and true crime author, spat.

I'd tripped over my mini goldendoodle, Agatha, three times already. Named after my favorite mystery writer, Agatha Christie, she clearly believed the name came with full sleuthing rights—rights that included darting underfoot at the worst possible moments, tail wagging like a suspect fleeing the scene.

On trip number one, the tepid tea had sloshed out of the blue Willowware teacup.

Trip number two, Veronica declared the tea tepid again and asked her husband, Dale, to come select a cup that didn't have a crack in it.

Trip three, I unplugged the reading lamp at the podium. Agatha had been munching on the cord when

I tripped over her, caught myself, and scooped her up before she could fry herself.

Veronica huffed over the disturbance. "Can no one fix the lighting here? It's like trying to do a reading in a chicken coop at midnight."

I'm sure the chicken comment referred to the excited clucking of the Maplewood Public Library book club attendees.

Mayor Silas Thorne was in attendance and bowed and scraped to Veronica by saying, "We are so honored to have such a highly esteemed author and literary genius grace us with her presence."

The Sleuths—Maplewood's amateur sleuthing crew who met every morning at the library, more reliably than most town committees—filed in behind the mayor, each man bringing his usual flair.

Thomas, still carrying the polish of a town councilman even in his scuffed loafers, tipped his hat. "Mayor. Always good to attend an event where the fiction's murder and not the budget."

James, booming and be-scarfed, gave a nod to Veronica Steele that managed to be both charming and challenging.

Randolph observed quietly, already studying the room as if someone had misfiled a body beneath the podium.

Antonio brought up the rear, suspenders stretched and voice rich with his trademark lilt. He squinted at Veronica's dramatic posture and muttered, "I thought James was our celebrity author." He scratched his chin. "Who is this lady?"

Thomas leaned in. "Veronica Steele. Crime fiction star. Big name—bigger ego."

Emory slipped in behind them, quieter than the others, hands tucked into his coat pockets, eyes already sweeping the layout like he was mapping a scene. Maplewood's new coroner didn't say much, but when he did, it came with the precision of a clinical observation—and the weight of a footnote that just might change everything. He lingered on the edge of the crowd like he wasn't sure if he was supposed to be at a murder investigation or book club, and honestly, in Maplewood, it could go either way.

Before the awkward silence could stretch any further—or Emory could back himself into a corner—the mayor stepped up to the cafe-style table we used as a podium and cleared his throat like he was about to deliver the State of the Union. The mayor, silver hair neatly parted and bifocals perched low on his nose, looked down at the crowd like every smile was a vote he intended to win.

"Maplewood, please join me in welcoming the incomparable Veronica Steele—bestselling author, master of mystery, and, if I may be so bold, the literary genius of our time."

When the mayor said "literary genius," James—Maplewood's celebrity novelist with fifty books under his belt—snorted and peeled away from the crowd.

Not his usual jovial self, he sequestered himself in a corner, brooding and sipping an espresso from the machine he'd donated to the library. He'd written his first novel here and had been a regular fixture ever since.

But today, his moody espresso-sipping routine was not helping my nerves. One more scowl from James and I was going to need an extra paper bag to breathe into.

Freda, creator of the Veronica Steele Fan-Girl site, host of the True Crime Lovers Podcast, was also a tripping hazard. Every time I tried to comply with Veronica's wishes— let's be honest...*demands*— Freda interjected herself into my space.

She'd stopped me in my tracks more than once with "Let me help you with that."

With one of those helpful moments, I'd turned too quickly and the Lorna Dune shortbread cookies on the requested Willowware China had slid off the plate and broken into pieces. I had been tempted to retrieve Agatha from my office and let her eat them so I didn't have to grab the broom.

Turns out, getting the broom from the closet had given me a brief respite.

I leaned against the door of the Children's Room, broom and dustpan in hand, weighing my options. I didn't dare bring out the vacuum. With Veronica's current list of grievances—tepid tea, subpar lighting, and general disruption—I had no doubt she'd consider it grounds for a formal complaint, possibly to the mayor, or the governor if she had the number.

"You okay?" Brandon leaned against the opposite doorframe, arms crossed, but his voice was soft. Real.

Not the clipped, cautious detective from his first days in Maplewood. This was the Brandon who noticed when I disappeared behind my smile. Who remembered how I liked my coffee and let the silence stretch until I filled it—on my terms.

He wasn't asking to be polite. He was asking because he'd been paying attention.

"I thought inviting a famous author would make the community happy." I adjusted my grip on the broom, already bracing for the irony.

"By community, you mean James, don't you?" Brandon's tone was dry, but not unkind.

"Yeah. He's been in a bit of a slump lately."

"Ever since Owen's first novel released."

I sighed. "I didn't realize authors were so competitive. I thought Veronica's reading would ignite his creative spark."

Brandon nodded, eyes scanning the hallway. "Well, if anything can jolt a person, it's Veronica Steele in full dramatic flair."

"Yoooohooo, Gabby," Angela, Library Director of the Grandview Library and book club, rounded the corner with a cup of coffee in her hand. She turned quickly when she saw us and the drink sloshed over the edge and onto the floor. "Oh, excuse me, I didn't…"

"I was just leaving," Brandon said as he followed my gaze to the coffee puddle. "I've got that, Gabby." He grabbed the broom and dust pan from my hands. "And the cookie crumbs too."

Angela gave me a crinkled disapproving look before continuing. "I don't think having a…whatever this was…" She stopped to peer into the Children's Room. "With a book club member…"

To say that Angela and I had a past wasn't accurate. She'd barely noticed my existence until Veronica had refused her invitation to speak at her book club and accepted mine instead. Since then, the emails and phone calls had been full of incessant reminders that Grandview was the more prominent library.

Yesterday's email had read:

Gabby,
I'm sure you'll agree that because my library is the more prestigious one that it makes sense that I intro-duce Veronica Steele. My van will arrive two hours before the author reading. Please suggest a dinner venue. Also, please be ready for my group with coffee and refreshments.
Grandview Head Librarian,
Angela Doty
Grandview Public Library,
The State's Premiere Library

The email signature boasted a professional photo of her in a tiny circle.

I'd responded:

Angela,
The Tasty Burger is a great restaurant.
I plan to do whatever Veronica wishes when it comes to introductions.
Gabby,
Maplewood Public Library

I'd included a small picture of Agatha in a tiny logo circle.

What Veronica had wished was for James to introduce her. Good thing I'd convinced him to stay. Whether he would follow through with her request was yet to be seen though.

I ignored the comment about meeting book club members alone in the Children's Room. "What can I help you with, Angela?"

She swooshed her auburn hair behind her shoulder with a flip of her hand. "I want to make sure my book club members get the premier seating."

"Angela, come on, I saved us some seats up front." Clarisa, Angela's best friend and co-conspirator, joined us.

I motioned back down the hallway. "We don't do assigned seats for book club events. It's pretty much first come, first serve."

Clarisa was a short squat version of Angela, with glasses too small for her round face. They both wore pants suits similar to Veronica's in autumn colors. Angela's burgundy pants accented her scarecrow like appearance with the too short pants. Clarisa's pumpkin orange pants bunched at the feet like a case of elephantiasis.

I glanced down at my autumn-hued plaid pants, burnt-orange cardigan, and trusty Doc Martens—all treasures from Second Time Chic. Maybe I should've gone with the pantsuit trend instead.

"You tell that crazed fan girl we get first dibs on the front row," Clarisa demanded.

"Freda can sit wherever she pleases." I couldn't believe I was defending Freda. But I'd had it with these two. The emails. The calls. The whole our-library-is-better vibe.

I led the way down the hallway while Clarisa continued to complain about Freda. "Did you see her thrift store pink pants suit? She's trying to *be* Veronica."

Angela replied, "Her latest podcast was about Veronica's new nonfiction book *The Best Villian Is The Worst Villian.*"

"I know," Clarisa returned. "She promised an interview with Veronica, as if that's ever going to happen." She stopped and guffawed with one hand on her stomach. When she realized we'd arrived back in the crowd of book club attendees, she straightened and made a beeline for the front row.

I chuckled. For as much as Clarisa and Angela claimed Freda was the crazed fan girl, they certainly devoted a lot of time to fan-girling — or maybe stalking — *her*.

I scanned the room for any new guests to greet. The cookie crumbs had already been swept away, and Brandon was deep in conversation with James and the rest of The Sleuths: Antonio, Randolph, Thomas, and Emory. James looked noticeably more at ease. When Brandon caught my eye, I mouthed a quiet "thank you."

Brittany tapped me on the arm. "Hey, Gabby, I want to introduce you to someone. This is Emily Stone. She's a writer as well."

Oh no, I said to myself. *More competition. And hello to you too. Way to chase a story instead of saying hello to your friend.*

"Hello to both of you." I stuck a hand out to Emily.

She smiled and gave me a hearty handshake. "Hello, I'm so glad I could come."

Emily looked to be in her mid-twenties, with masses of brunette curls streaked with warm gold highlights that caught the overhead lights just so. Slim and trendy, she had the effortless look of someone who somehow managed to throw on a blazer and graphic tee and make it look intentional. The tee read "Writers Do It Every Day" and below the slogan was an antique typewriter, the keys forming a faint heart shape.

"Veronica was Emily's writing coach for a few years," Brittany added.

"Oh, I didn't know she coached."

"Oh, yes," Emily said, tugging her blazer closed with one hand. "I really want to meet James Hatterson. Is he here?"

"He is the dapper gentleman in the group at the back."

She pivoted to the back of the room. "Thanks! Brittany, interview tomorrow? Where?"

"Daily Grind, at 9 am." Brittany pulled out her phone. "I just texted you the address."

I sighed. "Well, a fan of James. That will perk him up."

"You mean a young and gorgeous girl will give his ego a boost." She winked.

"She didn't ask where Owen was. That's a point in James's celebrity favor." Owen might not like too much attention, but lately he was getting it whether he wanted it or not. James had helped him along, though sometimes I caught a flicker in James's expression that made me wonder if he regretted creating his own competition.

.   .   .

Satisfied that James's ego was about to get a boost—and that he might trot Owen out just to remind everyone whose wing he'd come from—I went in search of Dale.

Dale, Veronica's husband, had given me a budget to spend on Veronica's must-haves, which made no sense since the library footed the bill. But who was I to question? I'd stuck to the budget, but only because I'd been able to score the cookies and tea from a discount outlet. The Willowware belonged to my friend Janet, who'd been murdered last year. Her son now managed her household belongings and had chosen not to sell it, but instead loan it out for tea parties and wedding showers. Since I'd proven his innocence in his mother's murder, not to mention having been a close friend with his mother, he'd allowed me to borrow it with no fee. Thankfully, the Lora Dune fan-girl disaster hadn't cracked the plate, and only the cookies were damaged.

"Oh, Dale, I was looking for you," I said as I bumped into him. "I have the printout of our expenses for your wife's appearance in my office."

"Thank you," he said through heavy jowls. "My wife thinks we are rolling in it," he finished with a huff.

I was sure he was referring to money, so I didn't ask.

As we left the common area and walked down the hallway to my office, he added, "These readings, as you people call them, actually lose money."

As I opened the door, Agatha bounded out. I'd have to get her later. Left to her own devices, she'd either be nosing around the snack table for stray cookie crumbs, tugging someone's shoelaces loose, or, worse, sneaking into the children's section to rearrange stuffed animals with her teeth.

"How so?" I asked.

"Public libraries love my wife. But we can't charge for these."

I picked up the expense report. "Does she want to charge?"

"Of course not. But we need to do more events that bring in income."

He studied the report and ran a pudgy hand over his face. "So this says, no charge."

"Nope. No charge. It's covered by the library."

"That other librarian from Grandview, what's her name?"

"Angela."

"Yes, her. She said the charge for my wife speaking was one thousand dollars. That's why I told her to choose this smaller library."

My eyes widened in shock, not because we were chosen based on our small size, but because Angela was charging the author when she had library funds at her disposal for an event like this.

"Sorry, no offense."

"None taken. I'm glad we were your choice, no matter how it came about."

He smiled, his face lighting up. "You're easier to work with than the other librarian." He ran his hand over his face again. "And my wife."

He opened his briefcase, which I hadn't noticed before. It must have been slung over his back with a strap. He slid the expense report in a folder.

"Has Veronica offered a lot of library-type readings?"

"She aims for a few a year," he admitted. "She's trying to 'meet the lesser fans.' Her words, not mine."

"It's fine. Celebrities, *right*? We have a few home-grown ones here tonight."

"Ah yes, James Hatteron. I love his books. Don't tell my wife though." He laughed. "He mentored her, but she won't give him the time of day."

That was news to me.

He snapped his briefcase closed and turned to leave, then paused.

"Maybe I should give you this."

He set his briefcase down and reopened it. He handed me a check.

"What's this?"

"A cashier check from the Veronica Steele Fan-Girl."

The check was for one hundred dollars.

"I can't take this. This is for your wife."

He took it back and stuffed it in his briefcase. "I think it's a bribe. Bert, Freda's boyfriend, slipped it to me when he came in. Then he asked me if Veronica would guest on Freda's podcast, True Crime Lovers."

"Is it standard to pay a fee to guest on a podcast?" I asked.

"Everything has a price." He turned and walked out.

I re-entered the main library just in time to see Owen step inside. He didn't look like a man craving notice—if anything, he seemed uneasy with the attention that now seemed to follow him everywhere. He was proud of his success, and rightly so, but it was strange to see him caught between the glow of recognition and the shadow it had cast over his friendship with James.

Only a year ago, he'd been the quiet man in a tattered army surplus jacket, clutching a battered brief-case and scribbling notes in his ever-present leather journal. He'd even fallen under suspicion once— wrongly accused of murder after what had turned out to be a very poorly executed attempt to protect me. It had been Brett, Janet's son and a psychologist, who had helped confirm what I'd begun to suspect: Owen was dyslexic. That revelation had explained so much, and with James's mentoring—trading the army jacket for dark jeans, a blazer, and a bit of polish—Owen had emerged with a new novel and more notice than he seemed to know what to do with.

And still, standing there, he looked like he'd rather blend into the bookshelves than bask in the spotlight.

Veronica made a beeline for Owen, her heels clacking across the hard library floor like an announce-ment in themselves.

"Oh my, handsome protégé," she purred, resting a manicured hand on his arm. "You must sit up front. What a success you are." *Protégé.* As if she'd discovered him in the wild and trained him up herself. Owen might have polished since those army-jacket days, but that had everything to do with his own work—and James's guidance—and nothing at all to do with Veroni-ca's fluttering eyelashes.

From my vantage point, I saw James stiffen. He'd stationed himself at the front near the podium, waiting to introduce Veronica, but the sight of her fawning over Owen set his jaw tighter than I'd ever seen it. James was rarely moody—flamboyant, dramatic, and occasionally insufferable, yes, but not broody. Watching him hover near the exit doors like a man plotting an escape route was…new.

When he finally angled toward the doors, curiosity tugged me forward, and I followed just close enough to catch what happened next. Brandon stepped neatly into James's path, blocking him with the kind of casual confidence that said he knew exactly what he was doing. His smile was polite, but deliberate.

"James," Brandon said, lowering his voice just enough that it carried only to the few of us nearby. "The library needs you. Gabby needs you. This community wouldn't be what it is without you."

For a heartbeat, James hesitated. His eyes flicked to Owen—still soaking in Veronica's praise—then back to me. Something unreadable passed across his face before his jaw tightened.

Finally, with a clipped nod, he muttered, "For Gabby and the library."

Behind us, Freda bustled forward with a fresh Willowware teacup. "Veronica, I made sure it's hotter this time." She beamed as she held it out.

Before Veronica could reach for it, Emily slid in out of nowhere and intercepted the cup, handing it over like she'd brewed it herself.

Freda froze, smile flickering. "I... made the tea," she said softly, her hands still outstretched.

Veronica accepted it like a queen accepting tribute. "At last. Someone competent."

Freda stepped back, blinking fast, like she'd just lost

her golden buzzer on *America's Got Talent* to a no-talent nobody.

Agatha growled softly at my feet. Not playful. Not even warning. Just unsettled—like she could already smell the trouble brewing.

James clapped his hands together, drawing everyone's attention. "Shall we get started?" he said, launching into a too-smooth introduction of Veronica and her many accomplishments.

Nobody noticed Veronica still holding the cup, or me locking eyes with her for a heartbeat too long.

For reasons I couldn't name, I felt a chill run down my spine.

CHAPTER 2

A KILLER READING

VERONICA ADJUSTED the microphone and read aloud, her voice rich and dramatic.

"The file was buried beneath a loose floorboard in the closet—police reports, a faded birth certificate, a hospital bracelet with a last name I'd never heard. No note. No explanation. Just twenty years of lies packed into a manila envelope. I sat on the cold hardwood, the bracelet in my hand, and realized the truth wasn't just hidden. It had been stolen. And whoever took me didn't expect I'd come looking."

She smiled, clearly impressed with her own prose. "That's from Chapter One of *Twenty Years Gone,* my upcoming bestseller."

Veronica raised the floral teacup like it was an Oscar. She inhaled the steam, paused for a beat too long, then took a sip.

Her face stiffened. She inhaled desperately before she spoke, voice tight. "That's... unusual."

She reached up and touched her throat, eyes wide.

"Is it warm in here?" She swallowed twice, slow and deliberate, like she was trying to talk herself out of whatever was happening.

The room seemed to hold its breath all at once, conversations snapping shut as if the whole library had leaned in at the same time.

Fingers trembling, she set the cup down, porcelain clinking—louder than I've ever heard in my life.

She clenched her other hand to her chest, brow furrowing.

That's when James started edging forward. I cut air into silent prayer.

"Veronica?" James asked softly.

She stood there, leaning slightly, her face paling into something almost… translucent. Her eyelids flickered, her breath turned shallow. Her designer shoes shifted, heels clicking on polished wood.

And then—snap!—her knees buckled.

Brandon lunged, hands flanking her like he meant to catch her.

I blinked as she collapsed, silent, onto the library floor.

Freda screamed— a sharp, jagged note rolling through the stunned hush of the audience.

Agatha barked once, percussive and urgent. She hopped toward the edge of Veronica's body, her little body shaking as if she sensed more than we did.

Veronica Steele—a queen of true crime—lay still at center stage, meaning the center of the library. No applause. No lights. Just questions.

Dr. Emory, our resident coroner, and Randolph— who never really stopped being the coroner no matter what his retirement papers said—rushed forward in one synchronized movement. Randolph barked out the order. "Step back, people."

The attendees did the opposite and surged forward as one mass amoeba. Freda continued to wail, holding her face with both hands while her boyfriend, Bert held her by the waist stopping her from rushing up to Veronica.

Detective Brandon took charge by barking, "Come on people. Let's move to the back of the room and find a seat. No one leaves."

"Is it…" Dale sputtered. "I mean…is she?"

Emory stood and faced Dale. "She's dead. Looks like poison. See the blue tint on her lips…"

I quickly joined Emory and gave him a jab in the ribs with an elbow.

"What?" He turned to me.

"He's the husband. A little bit of tact goes a long way."

"Of course." Emory turned back to Dale. "Your wife was poisoned, sir."

That was definitely not the tact I was referring to. I motioned to Angela and pointed to Dale. She dabbed her eyes with a tissue before taking a step in my direction.

"Clear this area," Randolph commanded. "This is officially a crime scene."

I gently led Dale to Angela and Clarisa, who apparently came as a pair. "If you two could sit with Dale. I think he is in shock."

"Should I make him a coffee with some sugar?" James asked, offering his standard cure-all for shock.

I turned and responded with, "Thanks, but I don't know if Detective Brandon will let you use the machine. This is a crime scene."

It had been less than a year since the library had been a crime scene. I'd been locked in the fishbowl room after book club, and almost hadn't made it out thanks to a candle laced with something far worse than a bad scent. Detective Brandon had shattered the glass and pulled me out just in time.

It had taken two months to replace the glass. I'd made sure the new lock didn't stick.

I shook my head. *Get a grip, Gabby. This wasn't the time to let old trauma take the wheel. You're the head librarian.*

People were looking to me—not just for books and story hour, but for steadiness when the unthinkable happened on the library floor. Veronica Steele was gone, and the last thing this room needed was me to fold in on myself. Order, calm, direction—that was my job now.

I wasn't extraordinary—unless you counted my knack for understanding human nature. Miss Marple had called it her only gift, and I'd borrowed that line more than once. Hopefully it would be enough tonight.

Detective Brandon nixed the coffee with sugar idea, but promised to have an officer bring one from The Daily Grind. With the sirens flashing outside the windows, I joined the rest of the Veronica Steele reading attendees in the Children's Room. Brittany had led them there with instruction from Detective Brandon. She was good at keeping her head when everything around her exploded into chaos.

Antonio tried his bulk on a plastic orange kid's chair and it creaked under his weight. As he hefted himself up with a hand from me, he said, "Gabby, another murder at the library. This is your third, yes?"

"It's not *her* murder," Thomas, former realtor and town councilman, defended me.

I gave him a nod of thanks and sat down on the floor cross legged. Agatha hopped on my lap and nudged my cardigan pocket which housed a few doggy treats for her. I pulled out a treat and fed it to her while I studied the suspects. Because let's just be honest here, everyone here was a suspect. Did everyone have a motive?

Her husband, Dale, sat in one of the few adult chairs with his head in his hands while Angela and Clarisa patted him on the back in unison.

Freda had calmed a bit and had settled down to a shuddery sob. She blurted out loud enough for everyone to hear, "I made her the tea. They are going to arrest me for murder and I," *sob* "loved her," * sob* "wouldn't murder her."

Bert reacted by shushing her and handing her a tissue. "Don't say anything more," he commanded.

Emily and Brittany had huddled up at an arts and craft table, which still displayed a Lego creation Ned, a story hour regular, had built earlier. As much as I wanted to hear what Emily had to say about her former writing coach, I didn't want to move. Agatha had settled enough to take a nap and I didn't want to wake her.

I knew what was next. Detective Brandon would question each of us. As if he read my mind, he appeared in the doorway and motioned for me. I stood, held Agatha like a rag doll and handed her to Antonio. He accepted her and held her like a sleeping baby.

"I need to use your office to question everyone." Brandon's voice was steady, all business, but his eyes lingered on me a second too long.

"I need to tell you some things I learned before tonight's reading." My hands twisted together at my waist, a nervous habit I'd never managed to break.

"No. Gabby." His tone softened, almost pleading. "You aren't sleuthing this time. Remember what happened last year." He shifted his weight, crossing his arms like he was trying to draw a line in the sand.

"I don't plan to go chasing murderers or get kidnapped this time." I adjusted my glasses and forced my chin up. "I just want to share what I learned."

He studied my face for a long moment, then reached out and brushed his fingers against my cheek, gentler than his original gruffness suggested. "I just don't want anything to happen to you."

"Am I interrupting something?" James asked as he squeezed into the doorway, carrying a drink carrier full of steaming cups.

"No, I'm just telling Gabby no Miss Marple-ing this time."

Antonio apparently had superman-like hearing because he responded with, "Detective, this is Gabby's *third* body at the library. Maybe this time she did it." He chuckled and his dough-like middle bounced Agatha awake. She leapt out of his arms and sniffed at Jame's shoes.

"Yes, my dear girl. I have donuts." James shifted his

gaze from Agatha and gave me a sympathetic look. "I don't think you murdered Veronica, Gabby, my dear." Then he strode into the Children's Room with the coffees and donuts holding them up like trophies. "I have sustenance my dear people."

Brandon and I walked down the hallway to my office, with me in the lead. I unlocked my office for the second time this evening.

"Do you want to hear what I found out?"

"Gabby… I need to interview everyone and get their statements."

"So you're brushing me off?" I'd grown a bit more backbone since I started dating Brandon—or maybe it started last year, when he arrested me and made me the star of the town gossip mill instead of simply asking for my help.

"No. I'm trying to follow procedure." He gave me a pleading look.

I kissed him on the cheek. "Coffee tomorrow with The Sleuths?"

"No, you aren't pulling them into Veronica's murder investigation."

"I think they're already *in* it." Before allowing him to reply, I added, "Who do you want first?"

"Angela. I'm sure she will want to head back to Grandview before it gets too late."

"Then you'll get Clarisa."

"What?"

"They seem to be connected at the hip."

"One at a time, please."

Back in the Children's Room, I found Angela and Clarisa munching on donuts while Dale sipped his coffee. I studied them. They didn't seem too upset that their favorite author was dead. Or was she really their favorite author? Maybe the whole Veronica-must-come-to-Grandview was all about something else. Something was fishy about these two and I couldn't put my finger on it.

Miss Marple always said people show you who they are by what they do when they think no one's watching. Right now, all I saw were donuts and very dry eyes.

"Angela, Detective Brandon would like to speak to you in my office. I'll take you."

She set down her napkin with half a donut on it and swallowed hard, her cheeks pinked. Was that guilt? Shame?

Clarisa set her donut down. "I'll come with you," she patted Angela on the back.

"The detective wants to interview you each...*separately*," I explained.

"May I walk back with you?" Clarisa asked.

"Of course." What else was I going to say?

Without any prompting, Clarisa added, "Angela has been struggling with panic attacks."

"Oh." I didn't know what to say. Like Miss Marple, I let Clarisa fill the silence.

"The job at Grandview Public Library has been stressful lately."

At this point, Angela turned and shushed her. "That's enough, Clarisa. You don't need to air all of my dirty laundry for this little small town librarian."

Although we'd arrived at the office door, I paused and tried another tactic. "Running a premiere library like Grandview must be stressful in and of itself."

"Yes, running Grandview, where we handle real programming, grant management, and state-level initiatives. I imagine Maplewood mostly runs itself with a few story times and book clubs, doesn't it?"

Detective Brandon opened the door, saving the library from a second crime. As she pranced in, I held my breath. As Miss Marple always said—*when people try to keep you out of things, it usually means they have something they'd rather you didn't see.*

CHAPTER 3
TICKET TO A MURDER

ANGELA AND CLARISA finished their statements and now sat bemoaning the fact *they* couldn't leave because everyone *else* still had to be interviewed.

James and Agatha made the rounds, trying to sooth ruffled feathers while I ushered people back to my office and then stood outside the door. I strained, with my ear against the door, to hear snippets of what interviewers reported.

"Listen, Mabel talked me into coming to see this Veronica person. I didn't care for her, but I didn't kill her," declared Bernice, a guest from Grandview, loud enough for half the room to hear. While I led her back to the Children's Room, she bemoaned the fact she'd spent the money to get on the van to come here this evening.

I stopped short and she almost plowed over me. "You paid to come here?"

"Of course, didn't everyone?"

"You mean you pitched in for the van's gas, right?" I

waited for her to respond as she clutched her handbag to her chest.

"No. We each paid one hundred dollars for our ticket." She unclasped her handbag and brushed a silver lock of hair from her face before digging around inside.

"Here it is." She produced a pink ticket with a one hundred dollar price and Veronica Steele in bold font.

"May I keep this?"

"Do I get my money back for tonight?"

"I'll see what I can do."

She shoved it in my hand and folded it over. "You're a sweetie. You asked about the van?"

"Yes." I paused and waited for her to reply.

"We had to pay for the ticket, our Airbnb, and our dinner, which is fine. The Tasty Burger is such fun. Reminds me of a place I used to go as a teen."

"Oh, I'm going to give her an earful. A murder. We each paid five hundred dollars. We don't have to watch this woman I didn't care for die right in front of us."

Detective Brandon stuck his head out the office door. "Gabby, are you getting…" He paused and looked at his list. "Mabel."

Bernice smiled, her cornflower-blue eyes locking on me.

I forced a polite smile back, though my gaze drifted —maybe a beat too long—toward Brandon. Whatever warmth flickered in his eyes steadied me more than I cared to admit.

"Oh, how sweet. You like him?" Bernice sing-songed before swinging her handbag and smacking Brandon square in the chest.

I ignored the question and asked one of my own.

"Detective, would you like to speak to Angela again?" I waved the ticket in the air like a flag.

"No. I'll take Mabel next."

"Angela charged one hundred dollars for each ticket."

"How many people came with you, Bernice?"

"Let me see. The van is a fifteen seater. Angela and Clarisa rode in the front. Joyce got sick at the last minute. Do you know Angela refused to refund her ticket…"

"Yes, that's interesting. That makes fourteen." Brandon honed his gaze on me. "I have to interview every one of them before anyone can leave."

"I see," Bernice said. She clutched her large purse to her chest, the knitting needles poked her ample chest, as she trotted down the hall. She turned her head and shouted, "I'll send Mabel back. You two stay here and…" She didn't finish her sentence, but said to herself, "Young love. Give me a romance novel…" and she was gone.

"Brandon," I said, addressing him informally, hoping I was being convincing and his dating me would get him to listen. "Angela charged each one of her patrons for a ticket as well as another four hundred dollars for this trip."

"So maybe larger libraries have bigger bills."

I bit back a reply. I knew libraries. They had funds for guest speakers and authors, but we didn't charge ticket prices for events like this. I swallowed and continued. "She isn't…"

Brandon interrupted with, "Mabel, thank you. This won't take long."

"Isn't this something? A real murder," Mabel said as she walked briskly down the hallway beside Brandon. Unlike Bernice's flustered excitement, Mabel was composed, her no-nonsense skirt and blouse as crisp as the faint lemon scent that trailed with her. She adjusted the strap of her sensible purse before adding, "That suave, debonair gentleman, James, says the head librarian here has quite the instincts."

Detective Brandon didn't need to support her arm. Instead he took a few quick long strides to keep up with her as she continued, "Did you hear she solved three murders in the past two years when that new detective couldn't do a thing?"

I leaned against the wall, enjoying his response and expression. He turned the color of a red maple in the fall and then turned to glare at me.

Mabel swallowed and sucked in her lips. "Oh it is you. The new detective. James didn't say you were so handsome."

He guided her in the office and shut the door with more force than necessary.

If he wasn't going to listen to me, I was going to find out what was going on with Angela and Grandview Library. Brandon could solve the murder on his own. I was going to save the integrity of the library system.

Once back in the Children's Room, I locked eyes with James, who was mid "my dear"-ing another Grandview guest.

I waved him over. "How is it going in here?"

"The natives are restless. If we don't start passing around wine or let them go, they may pull out their knitting needles and attack."

"Most of the Grandview guests are senior citizens, aren't they?"

"Yes, but don't worry, I'm mostly keeping them at bay." He straightened his collar.

"Yes, I've heard from several of them how debonair you are."

"Just doing my job. But you won't believe what I've learned."

"Same. Meeting of The Sleuths tomorrow?"

"So you want to solve the murder?"

"No, I want to solve the library scam."

"Yes, Bernice told me she practically emptied her bank account to come here."

"And yet she's excited to land in a mystery. She *is* a Miss Marple. Knitting bag included."

"Should we invite her to the meeting tomorrow?"

Agatha kangarooed up to my waist and I caught her.

"Yes, and Bernice too."

Agatha spotted Owen walking by with a half-eaten donut and lunged out of my arms to strut after him.

I shifted and asked, "How is Owen?"

"In shock. I honestly feel bad for him. I've been so clouded by jealousy that I didn't see he was floundering."

"He lit up when Veronica praised him." I nodded in Owen's direction. He was slumped on a chair with Agatha at his feet, begging for a cinnamon crunch donut. "Maybe you should talk to him and be liberal with the praise."

"You're right. I had no one to support me when my first novel was published, except Bea."

Bea was the former head librarian who had a no-nonsense teacher-like approach. She was in hospice now, after fighting cancer and her body losing the battle.

"She once told me that after you wrote your first novel, your father said 'now that you have that out of your system, are you going to get a real job.'"

"Sounds like exactly what Owen's dad said to him."

I gave James a quick hug and then he joined Owen. My phone buzzed. A text from Brandon:

I'm ready for Freda.

Oh boy. Freda's sobs had quieted. She huddled in a corner on a bean bag leaning on her boyfriend's chest. I squeezed through a few guests conversing to get to the corner.

I gently tapped her. "Detective Brandon would like to speak to you."

She uncoiled like a tight spring, shrieking simultaneously. "He thinks I did it, doesn't he? I mean, I would."

"Calm down, he just wants to question you."

"I can't go to jail. I'm claustrophobic."

Thomas came to my aid. "Freda, you must not say anything like that."

"Why not?" She scanned the room like a frightened rabbit.

"Because everyone will think you did it." He took her arm and led her through the throng.

"What you want to say," he continued, "is…"

He moved out of earshot, but whatever it was, it calmed her.

Bert unfolded himself and stretched. "Freda

wouldn't hurt a fly. She worships, I mean worshiped, Veronica."

"Make sure you tell Detective Brandon what you just said."

"Are there anymore donuts?" he asked in response, and lumbered off in the direction of the hastily arranged snack table.

I scanned the room. No Brittany. *Where was Brittany?*

"That twit," James whispered in my ear.

I thought he was talking about Bert, so I replied, "He doesn't seem upset that his girlfriend may have murdered her idol."

"Oh not *that* twit. I mean Owen. I may murder—strike that. I am not helping that ungrateful wretch."

"Let me guess, he reacted like a porcupine."

"Yes, and that's one set of quills I don't want to deal with right now."

Now wasn't the time to say Owen was triggered and reacting in a trauma response. Just like he did last year when he was diagnosed with dyslexia. He had put on an angry front and dressed in rag-like clothing. A defense mechanism.

"Where's Brittany?" I asked, changing the subject.

"Oh, Detective Brandon let her go. She needed to file a story."

"He let her go and we all have to stay here?"

My phone buzzed again.

I held up the screen for him to see.

"James, you are up."

"I see he saved the best for last," he replied and smoothed his shirt.

"Make it quick. Stick to the facts."

"Yes, Miss Marple." He patted me on the cheek. "None of this is your fault, Gabby. That woman…yes… the facts."

What were the facts? One of them was if James kept it short, we'd be out of here in ten or fifteen minutes.

I decided to take advantage of the time. I grabbed a donut and cold cup of coffee and seated myself next to the Grandview guests. Bernice was chattering and knitting at the same time.

"That cute little librarian in the plaid pants is some sort of super sleuth." It was then she noticed me sitting on the floor beside her. I'd just taken a swig of coffee when she turned, needles clacking away. "So who do you think did it?"

I choked on my coffee and coughed. She stopped knitting and patted me on the back.

I swallowed. "I am not solving the murder."

"Of course you are. From what I hear, you could solve it in your sleep."

"She throttled a murder with a smith corona typewriter," Mabel added.

The three women in the group looked at me with wide-eyed admiration.

"And she is in love with the detective," Bernice added as she went back to knitting. "But he doesn't listen to her."

"Typical man," Mabel added.

I swallowed and switched the subject. "I'm more interested in the tickets you had to buy to attend the author reading."

Agatha climbed on my lap and licked the crumbs off my pants.

"What a cutie," Bernice said.

In response to the compliment, Agatha hopped up and licked her Mary Jane-style shoes.

"She likes me," Bernice dropped her knitting on her lap and leaned over to scoop Agatha up. The next five minutes were spent cooing over Agatha.

Doris leaned over and patted Agatha. "This little dog here solved a murder by licking the murderer's shoe."

"And she almost died," Bernice added.

I wasn't getting anywhere with the library instigation into Angela's money scams.

I stood as James and Detective Brandon rejoined us.

"Everyone you are free to go," Detective Brandon said with his hands on his hips. "Don't leave town."

It was then I noticed James's hands were behind his back.

As he passed us, I saw the cuffs.

I stood in front of the door to block their way.

"What are you doing, Brandon?"

"James is under arrest for the murder of Veronica Steele."

"You can't be serious."

"Gabby, stay out of it. This is police business."

I caught James's eyes. Was that fear? Or guilt.

"Help me," he mouthed.

The Grandview ladies swarmed around me like a flock of ruffled hens.

"James?" Mabel gasped. "He wouldn't hurt a fly!"

"He helped me down the library steps when my knee gave out," Doris said. "Didn't even know me."

"Besides," Bernice whispered loudly, "if anyone

around here looked guilty, it's that Freda girl. Always skulking around in the background. Clutching that giant purse like she's smuggling a library archive."

My eyes darted toward the edge of the room.

There she was.

Freda—Veronica's frenzied fan club president—edged toward the side door like she didn't want to be noticed. Her bright pink suit shimmered with every step, and her matching Converse flashed like warning lights.

Everyone else was staring at James. But I couldn't take my eyes off Freda—still trembling, still wide-eyed, still clutching her oversized purse like it held more than tissues and a crumpled program.

She'd cried the loudest, wailed the longest, and made the biggest scene.

But I'd read enough mysteries to know: It's not always the one who hides... it's the one who hides in plain sight.

And Freda? She wasn't shrinking back anymore. She was trying to slip away.

Funny thing, I thought, watching her inch toward the door. *"Grief makes you weep. Guilt makes you flee."*

CHAPTER 4
GROUNDS FOR SUSPICION

THE NEXT MORNING, there was no reason to open the library. It was a crime scene. I drove by in my buttercream VW Bug on the way to The Daily Grind, where The Sleuths had decided to meet.

The perimeter of the library was swathed in yellow crime scene tape. Third time in three years. Take that, Angela—we don't just have book clubs and story hours. We have murders too.

I tapped my foot on the brake, and Agatha protested with a sharp bark from the passenger seat.

Why in the world did I think a murder was a point for Maplewood Public Library?

I supposed my Miss Marple was shining through.

I pulled into the parking lot and waved at Brittany, who responded by jogging over to my car.

"The Sleuths are meeting here?" she asked, even though she knew the answer to the question.

"Yep, and Thomas is picking up Mabel, Doris, and Bernice, our honorary guests."

"Honorary guests, my foot." Brittany reached in the open door and scooped up Agatha. "You're investigating."

"Yes, I am. But not the murder."

"You're just leaving James rotting in a jail cell?"

"James didn't murder Veronica, and you know it."

Before I could say anything further, Thomas pulled up in his gold Volvo and honked as he parked next to me. The three guests of honor, as I'd called them, clucked like happy hens being released from the henhouse. Finally free range, and they were making the best of it.

"You need to Google James and Veronica," Brittany said as she handed me Agatha.

Thomas helped Bernice out of the front seat and handed her the handbag with her knitting needles, the one she'd been carrying last night. "I'd Google him myself, and if only I was five years younger…"

"Bernice, you are eighty-five," Mabel clipped as she exited the backseat.

"So?"

Doris added, "Reporter lady means Google on a computer, not ogle."

The three continued their banter as Thomas led them into The Daily Grind.

"I'll be there in a minute," I called after Thomas.

"Sorry, gotta run. Meeting Emily. Catch up later, and we can compare notes."

Agatha and I were alone in the parking lot. I pulled out my phone, and it automatically logged into The Daily Grind's Wi-Fi. I Googled "James Hatterson and

Veronica Steele." Several articles popped up with a younger version of James, looking as dashing as ever in a white button-down and charcoal gray slacks. Veronica was a great deal younger, with wide eyes and fresh dewy skin. One headline read:

Famous Author Steals From Veronica Steele, Claims Young Prodigy

I continued to read:

In a shocking literary scandal, rising star Veronica Steele has accused bestselling author James Hatterson of plagiarizing her unpublished manuscript. Steele arrived at the publisher's Manhattan office flanked by her legal team and her father, asserting that Hatterson passed off her words as his own. While the publishing house declined to press charges, the fallout was immediate—book deals stalled, reputations were shattered, and Hatterson withdrew from the public eye.

The article answered some questions and raised some new ones.

"Aren't you going in?" Antonio asked as he patted Agatha on the head. For a large man, Antonio had an amazing ability to sneak up on people.

"Yes, let's go in together." I slid my phone in my pocket and linked arms with him.

"It's too bad about James. I don't think he murdered Veronica." He opened the door to The Daily Grind and paused to let me go first.

The pungent smell of coffee filled my nostrils and reminded me of James. "I don't think so either."

"Then why are you crying?"

"I don't know."

I didn't have time to process the article or my emotions. Bernice waved a knitting needle at us from a corner booth. "Yoohoo!"

"I'll order for you...and you." He patted Agatha's head. "You go join them."

Thomas was in line already. I'm sure he was ordering for the rest of The Grandview ladies.

Agatha led the way, stopping to lick Brittany's shoes. I kept going, and she caught up.

Emory and Randolph swooshed by me, talking about the crime scene. They were so engrossed in their conversation they didn't see me.

"The victim was poisoned," Emory was saying. "We're getting the teacup tested, of course."

"Who made the tea?"

"Gabby, I assume."

They'd arrived at the table where Bernice sat, knitting and listening. They paid no attention to her. It was time for me to burst their coroner-bubble before they said something they'd regret. Bernice might've been sitting quietly, waiting for Thomas to bring her coffee, but in an alternate reality, she'd already landed the lead in a mystery novel—preferably as Miss Marple, armed with knitting needles and highly classified super-hearing.

"I'm right here, guys."

Agatha trotted up behind me and nudged Emory as

if she knew he had no filter and it was her job to stop him.

Bernice continued her knitting, her needles clacking away. Probably hoping they would start talking about the murder again.

I slid in the booth and said, "Hello, Bernice. You remember Randolph and Emory."

"Can't say that I do. Were you two at book club last night?"

"Yes, I'm the county coroner," Emory said, as he slipped in on the other side.

"Is that so? And you, sir?"

"Retired county coroner." Randolph stuck out a hand to shake.

Bernice probably knew this—if she were playing Miss Marple, I was sure of it. She was more sleuthy than she let on.

"I'll go and order our coffees," Randolph offered.

"Antonio is taking care of Agatha and me."

"That nice young man, Thomas, is ordering—"

Before she could finish, Thomas, Doris, and Mabel returned. Thomas set the tray of coffees down and grabbed a few extra chairs to add to the table.

I opted for sliding out of my position and sitting in a chair so I could exit quickly in case Agatha decided to visit other tables.

Thomas leaned over and whispered in my ear, "These ladies haven't stopped talking since I picked them up at their Airbnb."

"I'm sorry," I whispered back.

"No. Don't be. I've learned some pretty interesting

things I'll share at our next official meeting of The Sleuths, sans…them."

"I have a feeling Mabel and her friends aren't leaving town until the mystery of who murdered Veronica is solved," I said, half to myself. "They'll probably name it something dramatic… *Death at the Author Reading* has a certain ring to it."

Thomas straightened his tie. "So I should share what they learned so you can get James off the hook."

I hoped Thomas was on the James-is-innocent side. "You don't think he killed Veronica, do you?"

"Do you know their history?"

"A little." By a little, I meant I'd read a headline of an article and a few sentences.

"You can ask him yourself and see what you think."

"How?"

"He's here." Thomas pointed to the entrance.

James stood in the middle of the cafe scanning the tables. I waved and called, "Over here, James." Agatha ran like a crazed puppy, dashing over feet and between legs until she arrived in front of him. She hopped and yapped until he picked her up.

James was still wearing the clothes he'd worn to the author reading the night before. The shine of his normally dapper appearance had been scrubbed off and replaced with a haggard face and rumpled clothes. He held Agatha at his chest as he maneuvered the crowd with his head down. No "hellos" or "my dears." The march of a man heading for the gallows, with a puppy he held onto for dear life.

"I'll go grab you your usual," I offered.

"Could I speak to you privately?" he asked, still clutching Agatha.

Thomas stood. "I'll get your order, James. Go talk to Gabby."

James led me to a table in the corner, away from the hens and The Sleuths. We passed Angela and Clarisa on our way to a table in the corner. He set Agatha down, and she licked his shoes.

"Your detective thinks I murdered Veronica because of our…" He paused. "History."

"You mean the history where she accused you of stealing her work."

"Yes, that."

"And did you?"

He ran a hand over the stubble on his face. "Leave it to you, my dear, to always be the sleuth."

"I can't imagine you'd wait twenty years to kill someone who…" I put a hand on his. "I'm sorry I invited her here. I thought you'd enjoy having another bestselling author to swap stories with."

He chuckled. "Bad choice of words."

Thomas arrived with our coffees and a doggy treat for Agatha. James took a sip of his coffee and scanned the room. I followed his gaze as his eyes landed on Brittany.

"Do you think we could invite Brittany over? It's time I told my side of the story."

Brittany was still chatting with Emily, probably getting the scoop about how wonderful Veronica was. I waved her over. She made some sort of excuse to Emily and joined us.

"Sorry to interrupt your interview."

"It's okay. Emily is upset over Veronica's death, like the rest of last night's attendees."

Were they though? No one else at The Daily Grind seemed too broken up by her murder. The hens were busy laughing and flirting with The Sleuths. Clarisa and Angela hunched over steaming coffees and cinnamon rolls, deep in conversation. No tears for Veronica.

Brittany plopped down next to me, stowing her backpack on the back of the chair. "So what's up?"

James set his coffee on the table. "I want to tell my side of the story. About Veronica and the manuscript."

"You want to set up a formal interview?"

"How about I give you the basics now, and we can meet later after I get cleaned up?"

"Works for me," Brittany said. "I'd planned to run Emily's story as well as what was going on in the investigation, tomorrow. But with Emily clamming up, half of that is down the drain."

"You mean you're running the story *Famous Local Author Arrested for Murder* along with the bylines from twenty years ago?"

"Sorry, James, it's not personal."

"I understand. You're the press. It's your job. That's why I want to share my side of the story."

I wanted to hear James's side of the story. I did. But I also wanted to catch Angela and Clarisa before they left. I'd promised myself I wouldn't investigate Veronica's murder, and surely Detective Brandon would have another suspect in custody by the end of the day. James would be in the clear.

"You two keep talking. I'll be right back." I squeezed out from my place at the table, and Agatha followed, sniffing the ground for any scraps of gooey cinnamon roll or muffin.

Angela and Clarisa were deep in conversation, forehead to forehead. They were dressed in similar pantsuits again, one in marigold, the other violet, looking like a pair of autumn leaves. Angela, tall and scarecrow-like, looked windblown and sharp. Clarisa looked crumpled, like her suit had folded in on itself—and maybe she had too.

"Ladies, mind if I join you for a minute?"

Angela jerked her head up. "Oh, hello, Gabby. It is a shame your little library is out of commission."

"Because it's a crime scene," Clarisa added.

"Our library has never been a crime scene."

"There was the one time…"

Angela gave Clarisa a look that snapped her mouth closed.

"I just wanted to ask you a question about the tickets to attend Veronica's reading."

"What about them?"

No one offered me a seat, so I stood awkwardly in the middle of the aisle while Agatha munched on a chunk of cinnamon roll one of them had dropped.

Angela adjusted her marigold blazer like she was straightening battle armor. "The tickets are perfectly legal, Gabrielle. West Virginia Code 10-1-9A. Libraries are permitted to establish reasonable fees for programs deemed beneficial to the community."

I tucked my hands behind my back to keep from fidgeting, mostly because Agatha's cinnamon roll crumb chewing was echoing like a guilt trip across the tiled floor. "I'm sure you've memorized the code in your spare time." My voice stayed light, but my pulse gave an uneven skip. "But doesn't it seem…well, just a touch unethical to charge people to come into the public library? It's supposed to be a refuge. Not—" I waved a hand at the crowd packed shoulder to shoulder, lingering over half-empty coffee cups like it was the afterparty to a crime scene, "—an exclusive club with a cover charge."

Clarisa snorted softly, but Angela's lips twitched in what I guessed was supposed to be a smile. It missed the mark by a country mile.

"Maintaining quality events requires funds," she countered, smoothing her blazer again. "I'm sure your…modest branch will catch up to Grandview's standards one day."

A shard of cinnamon roll stuck to Agatha's chin like a badge of rebellion. I focused on brushing it off instead of voicing the list of things I wanted to say.

We might not charge admission, I thought, *but at least our staff doesn't resemble fall foliage arguing over ethics.*

I smiled instead. The quiet kind. The Miss Marple kind that gathered every detail for later.

"Thank you, Angela. That's very illuminating."

Agatha sneezed cinnamon dust all over my boot, and I took it as our cue to retreat.

James was gone.

I motioned to where he'd sat. Agatha took my hand motion as a cue to hop on his vacant seat. "What happened?"

"Detective Brandon wants to ask him some more questions. He went home to shower and change before going back to the police station."

I sat down and picked up my coffee. It was cold. I felt as if I were spinning my wheels. Nothing made sense. Dale had said Veronica was spending more money than they made. Clarisa was charging for tickets to an event at my library, draining the hens' bank accounts, and not apologizing for it. Maybe, to speak in Agatha's language, I was barking up the wrong tree.

I was focusing on money instead of murder.

CHAPTER 5

FOLLOW THE MONEY NOT THE MURDER

THE CROWD at The Daily Grind thinned out. Thomas gathered the hens and returned them to their Airbnb for a rest. By that, I meant rest for him. I can imagine Mabel snoozing with one eye open while still listening and absorbing everything going on around her.

With the rest of the day off, I left my car parked at The Daily Grind and took a walk to admire the foliage and think. Agatha needed to walk off the cinnamon roll just as much as I needed the fresh air to sort through my thoughts. Walking would check both boxes.

I snapped the leash on her harness and stepped out the door into the crisp air. We walked past the library, still wrapped in crime scene tape as if a toddler had gift-wrapped it. No story hour today. I'd miss the kids and their enthusiasm, and I wondered what new game Ned was playing this fall. When we arrived at the gazebo in the middle of the town square, I sat down on a bench. Agatha sat at my feet.

"Good morning Gabby." Freda plopped down on the bench next to me. Freda had ditched her bright pink suit for a crop top and jeans.

Before I could say hello, she burst into tears and between sobs added, "I still can't believe Veronica is dead."

"Oh there you are," Bert said, coming up from behind us.

"Hello, Bert."

By this time, I was awkwardly patting Freda on the back while Agatha licked her shoes to comfort her.

"I told her to take a walk to calm her down. She didn't make it far." He motioned to the old- fashioned motel across the street from the gazebo.

"I'm sorry. I'm so upset," Freda explained, and then pulled out a tissue and blew her nose with a loud honk.

Bert sat on the bench next to me and reached over and patted Freda on the knee."I don't know why you're so broken up about that witch's death."

Freda honked into a fresh tissue and added, "She was amazing. I was her number one fan."

Bert turned to me, the icing in this comfort session oreo. "Veronica treated her like sh—." He paused. "She treated her very badly."

"In what way?" I asked. I hadn't had time to observe any interactions between the two last night, other than Freda delivering the tea.

"Well, Freda does all this free marketing for her, you know. On the podcast, social media. I'm kind of a numbers guy."

"And you've tracked it?"

Freda continued to sob softy. Agatha took this a cue

to hop on her lap and snuggle up. Freda patted her and blew her nose again.

"Yeah, I've got the data. I've tracked it since Freda started her podcast and Instagram account."

He pulled out his phone, tapped the screen a few times, and held it up. A graph lit up. "These are her book sales before Freda started the podcast."

He directed me to a red line. It stretched across the screen in a flat-line.

"So before Freda started her podcast, Veronica's book sales were flat-lined."

"Yeah. Pretty much like dead on the table." He scrolled to another graph. "This green line is after the podcast launch."

The green line ascended in jagged peaks.

"And check out her Insta." He clicked on another icon and showed me the account– all about Veronica. "Look how many followers."

I leaned in to see the number. "Is that 100,000?"

"Nope. It is one million. People all over the world."

"Is Veronica in any of those little videos?"

Freda sniffed. "They are called reels. I film two a day. All about her books. Her characters."

"And to answer your question, no. Veronica is not. Check out Veronica's Insta."

He clicked on her account. "Fifty thousand followers."

Freda reached over and grabbed the phone, scrolling like a woman possessed. "And zero reels. Just stuff the publisher marketing department posted."

She held the phone two inches from my face before jerking it back. I caught a brief glare of the screen, then nothing. She read aloud in a monotone, like the automated voice on my GPS—right after the turn I missed.

"Another Gripping Mystery from Bestselling Author Veronica Steele. Available Now," she recited, deadpan.

I groaned. "Wow. That screams fun and approachable."

Freda kept scrolling. *"Preorder the Latest Installment in the Acclaimed Veronica Steele Series Today,"* she droned, eyes wide in mock horror. "Seriously? Did they pull these out of a 1990s PR manual?"

"Apparently," I muttered, snatching the phone to see for myself. The third post loomed like a funeral announcement.

"New Release: The Latest Novel by Award-Winning Crime Writer Veronica Steele," I read, mimicking her robotic delivery.

Freda flopped back on the bench. Agatha hopped down and ran in circles at her feet.

"How does someone with millions of readers make murder sound this boring?"

"Talent," I said, handing the phone back. "That, or a really aggressive marketing intern with no personality."

"So, as I was saying," Bert continued. "The numbers don't lie. Freda saved Veronica's career."

I looked at Freda. "Did she thank you?"

"Thank her?" Bert laughed. "Veronica answered zero of Freda's one thousand emails."

"I came last night to ask her personally to guest on my podcast."

"And…" I waited for her to continue as I scooped up Agatha.

"She said no and could I please get her a fresh cup of tea and…"

"Make sure it isn't tepid," I finished for her.

"Yes! How did you know?"

"She said to me, 'You call this tea hot? It is tepid, that is what it is.'" I tried my best to imitate her voice.

"That's exactly what she said to Freda."

My sleuth brain switched on. "Was she sipping tea?"

"Yes, she took a sip before she handed me the fancy cup."

Freda and Bert could've murdered her. I might be, at this very moment, the cream icing in a murderer sandwich. While Detective Brandon was questioning an innocent man, *again*, I was sitting in the town square outside the gazebo with a pair of poisoners.

Don't panic, Gabby. Ask a few more questions.

"Did you make the tea?"

"Oh no," Freda said. I asked that other famous author, the young one, to make it.

"Did he?"

Bert chuckled. "No. He didn't seem too competent with it. He poured the tea leaves right in the cup."

"So did you?"

"No. Freda asked me to film so she could make a few reels from the reading."

"So who made the tea?"

"Honestly, I don't know. The young author…"

"Owen," I filled in for him.

"Yeah, he promised to find someone and five minutes later, he gave Freda the steaming hot cup."

So, either Freda added something to it before he delivered it or someone else did.

No. No. No. Gabby, you aren't not investigating. James will be in the clear by the end of the day. Detective Brandon was competent and capable of handling this investigation.

I stood, sending Agatha scrambling off my lap."It was nice chatting with you."

Freda pulled a fresh tissue out of her oversized handbag. "I don't know what I'm going to do…"

I wasn't sure if she meant what she was going to do about being arrested for murder, or what she was going to do now that her entire career of building up Veronica Steele's empire was circling the drain. Either way, the woman looked seconds from unraveling. My inner Miss Marple reminded me that people rarely fall apart for the reason they *say* they're falling apart. It's usually the quiet, creeping disaster beneath the surface that tips them over the edge.

And I had a sinking feeling Freda was standing on the edge of more than one cliff.

———

I left Freda and Bert sitting on the bench and walked back to my car in The Daily Grind parking lot. I was about to unlock it and drive home, when I spied Dale inside, sitting alone, nursing a cup of coffee.

I promised myself I'd follow the money trail, not the murder. Sure, Detective Brandon was grilling an innocent man – James – again, but he'd get around to questioning Freda and Bert, right?

"Mind if I sit down?" I asked as I approached the table.

"I could use some company," Dale answered as he motioned to a seat. "Let me grab you a coffee."

"I never say no to coffee." I slid my coat off, draped it over a chair and sat. I looped Agatha's leash around the leg of the table. She'd had enough cinnamon roll to burst her stomach. I fed her a doggy treat.

Dale stood. "What would you like?"

"I'll take a coffee with heavy cream." I'd had enough espresso today.

He shook his head and went to the counter.

Agatha settled down for a nap as I scanned the empty dining room.

Dale slid a coffee across the table toward me. The mug read "**Deja Brew**," which felt appropriate considering I'd been here once already today, running in circles—physically and mentally. With his other hand, he set down a pumpkin muffin topped with a generous crumble of brown sugar.

"I thought you could use this," he offered awkwardly, like a man who hadn't quite decided if he was making conversation or dodging a crime scene.

"Thanks." I wrapped my hands around the mug, grateful for the warmth, if not the growing suspicion curdling my insides.

Agatha curled under the table, content for now. I wasn't so lucky.

Dale settled across from me, eyes scanning the nearly empty cafe like he wasn't sure if someone might overhear. "Did you hear about the will?"

I paused, coffee halfway to my lips. "The will?"

"Veronica's."

I let out a soft huff of disbelief.

Dale continued, his eyelids heavy—grief, or maybe anger. "Veronica updated her will. I just found out when her lawyer contacted me. Twenty-four hours ago she was planning book tours and ordering tea like royalty, and now this?"

I took a sip of my coffee for two reasons—to study him and to gauge what this meant concerning Veronica's murder—before asking, "You didn't know she planned to change her will?"

"I did not." His jaw twitched like the words tasted sour. "I'm named in it."

I tilted my head, studying him the way Agatha studies squirrels—polite curiosity laced with suspicion.

"She left me half of what's left," he added, bitter.

"And what's left?"

"Not as much as I'd like." He stirred his coffee, eyes distant. "She drained her accounts the past few years. Quiet payments. To people…who didn't exactly show up on any official payroll."

I kept my face neutral, but my brain cataloged every syllable like library inventory. Quiet payments? Ghost expenses? That wasn't "eccentric author" behavior— that was…something else.

"And the other half?" I asked.

His lips pressed into a thin line. "James"

"James?"

"The man she always claimed had stolen her work." Dale's brow furrowed.

I raised an eyebrow. "That seems…sudden."

"There's a clause," Dale muttered, tapping his spoon against the saucer. "The money's tied up unless James jumps through a few hoops. Veronica loved hoops. Power games, control—same old story."

Agatha let out a soft sigh from under the table, oblivious to the slow unraveling happening above her.

My internal Miss Marple—the one I usually tell to hush and stick to shelving books—leaned in. Quiet payments. Money vanishing. An inheritance with conditions.

And James—the accused, staring down an unexpected payday.

I wasn't investigating. I was walking my dog. Drinking coffee. Asking harmless questions.

Except harmless questions have a way of breeding bigger, messier ones.

I drained the last of my coffee, the warmth doing nothing to thaw the chill curling down my spine.

"One more question," I muttered to myself, slipping Agatha's leash back into my hand. "Just one more."

But we both knew I was lying.

CHAPTER 6
SLEUTH MODE IGNITED

DALE EXCUSED himself and went back to his hotel room.

I was in full-on sleuth mode now. There were too many people who had a motive to kill Veronica. I made a mental list: Dale, Freda, Bert, Emily – last on the list, James. I didn't think James did it but Detective Brandon did so it was important to include James on the murder board.

Murder board. Yep. Fully committed. But where could I set it up? The library was a crime scene. The Daily Grind was out of the question. They may appreciate the business, but not a murder board in the middle of the cafe.

I texted Emory.

When can we get back into the library?

I knew the text should have gone to Detective Brandon, but I couldn't bring myself to talk to him. Deep down I knew he was doing his job and following the clues he had in front of him. But like Miss Marple, I knew gathering clues by watching and listening outside the police station were more effective. I mean, how many times could he ask James the same questions and get the same answers?

I imagined James sitting under a glaring light, running his fingers through his silver hair, rehashing history from twenty years ago.

Emory texted back.

> It will be all clear tomorrow.

Oh good. That was fast. Too fast.
I texted him back:

> Why so quickly?

He returned.

> James has been officially charged. His DNA was all over the crime scene. Plus he has motive.

I was too angry to answer. Of course James' DNA was all over the cafe-grade equipment he had donated to the library. Not to mention he'd help me unpack the Willowware and expensive tea Veronica had demanded.

I picked up the sleeping Agatha and exited the Daily Grind, bypassing my car and marching straight for the police station. Agatha trotted beside me, enjoying the crisp air and the pace. Occasionally, she took off after a leaf whirling around in the air, but the harness halted her.

I pulled her back on the sidewalk. "Sorry girl, I'll let you chase leaves later at home."

By the time I reached the police station, I'd worked up a sweat—and a simmering anger to match. I pushed through the door, gave Desk Sergeant Bob a nod, and said, "I need to see Detective Brandon."

"What's up Gabby?" he asked as he breezed through the door from the official part of the police station.

"What's up," I hissed through gritted teeth, "is that you arrested James for a murder he didn't commit."

"I know you're upset, Gabby. But all the evidence points to him."

Agatha yipped in disagreement as if she understood what Detective Brandon was saying.

"And how did you know I'd officially charged him? Nevermind. Emory."

Of course it was Emory. He and I had a special sort of friendship, forged through The Sleuths. He never paid much attention to social boundaries—or police protocol. If he knew something, I knew it too.

"Yes, I asked him when I could get back in the library. He seems to think you have the case wrapped up."

He crossed his arms in a defensive stance. "I do."

"Can I see him?"

"For a few minutes." He waved his arm in the direction of the interview room.

I handed him Agatha's leash and brushed past him.

I opened the door. No bright light. James was

sipping a cup of coffee. He wore a resigned, haggard expression.

"Oh my dear, thank you for coming."

I shut the door and slid into a chair.

"Are they watching?" I eyed the cameras.

He didn't answer my question. "So this is how my successful career ends. A murder. How apropos for a mystery writer. I couldn't have written it better myself."

"I know you didn't murder her."

"It doesn't matter what you think. Just like it didn't matter twenty years ago when she published my manuscript as hers...and won the court case."

"Wait. What? There was a court case?"

"No. I didn't want my reputation slashed through the courts, so we settled out of court."

"You paid her."

He leaned forward and held his head in both hands. "You could say I ignited her career while mine fizzled out."

"And you came back to Maplewood and lived in obscurity."

"Yes, that's how I thought of it at first." He sat up straighter. "Later I changed my mind. It was the best decision I ever made."

"For your career?"

"No. Not exactly. For me, really. Having real solid friendships trumps hotel hopping and clawing up the rankings every time."

"Yet, you hit the bestseller list over and over."

"Much to Veronica's chagrin."

"Why would she care?"

"She had to be the best, no matter how she got there.

Whether she stole someone else's work or schmoozed the right people to get the ratings."

"Oh." I paused and thought of what Dale had said about her finances. What was it?

"She drained her accounts the past few years. Quiet payments. To people…who didn't exactly show up on any official payroll."

James pulled a handkerchief out of his pocket and wiped his forehead. "Gabby, there is something I need to tell you."

I leaned forward, hoping it was some evidence to exonerate him.

"Veronica and I had an argument before the reading."

"Really? When? Where?"

I searched my memory banks for a time when both she and he were out of my sight.

"When you were back in the Children's Room washing the Willowware in the sink."

"But that didn't take long."

"Neither did the argument."

"What did you say?"

"You mean, what did she say to provoke me?" He fiddled with a handkerchief before continuing. "She jabbed her finger into my chest and said, 'Who's the bestseller now? Even your little secondhand-clothing librarian chooses me.'"

He paused.

"And what did you say?"

"I told her I was going to go public and tell everyone she stole my manuscript."

"You were?"

"Yes, Brittany was going to write the piece."

I patted him on the hand. "She still can."

"I'm sure she's already crafting a completely different piece with a headline like 'Top Crime Novelist Slays Rival at Live Event—Literally.' And somewhere in the third paragraph, she'll casually remind the world that twenty years ago, James Hatterson settled out of court after accusing Veronica Steele of swiping his manuscript. Because nothing sells papers like old scandal, recycled with a body count."

I couldn't argue with him. I knew Brittany, and the story was important to her, maybe more important than friendship or fact. But there was more to the story than James or Brittany knew. From what he'd told me so far, which made no sense, considering Veronica's new will. He didn't know he was a beneficiary. If so, Veronica was feeling guilty. So why still treat him as if he were second rate.

The door opened, and Detective Brandon stepped in, eyes flicking to James before landing on me. His jaw tightened ever so slightly—the way it always did when he thought the hard part was over.

"Times up, Gabby." His tone was gentle, but his posture screamed *I've got this under control*, which was ironic, considering he currently had the wrong man in custody.

I stayed seated a moment longer, not ready to abandon James to his fate or let Brandon's stubborn certainty go unchallenged. Was it totally wrong that I didn't mention Veronica's new will? Yes. But I wasn't about to give him more evidence in the "James did it" file. He was a detective. He could find out about the will on his own. But then he did it—the one-two punch that always complicated things.

He handed me Agatha, curled up like a cinnamon roll in his arms, fast asleep and blissfully unaware that dinner plans were about to come with a side of suspects. His hand brushed mine as I took the leash, lingering for a beat too long. Warm, steady, protective. Everything I wanted.

And completely infuriating.

"Still up for dinner tonight?" he asked, his voice softening in that way that always made me forget, momentarily, that I wanted to throttle him.

Brandon and I had been dating long enough for me to recognize the pattern: murder, tunnel vision, wrong suspect—including me once—followed by an awkward dinner where we pretended everything wasn't unraveling around us.

And yet, the look in his eyes—the quiet concern behind the detective bravado—always caught me off guard. He cared. I knew that. He just didn't always trust me.

"Sure," I answered, forcing a smile. "The Tasty Burger?"

If he wasn't going to listen to me directly, I'd just have to let dinner do the talking. I had suspects to nudge, conversations to steer, and a town full of loose threads to unravel.

Let him think this case was wrapped up neat and clean.

I knew better.

Okay, so I had a plan. The way I got Detective Brandon to trust me in the past was to let other people lead the way. By that, I meant talk in front of him. Act like suspects in front of him. My first stop before going home was the Airbnb the hens were staying in to prod them into coming to dinner. Then make sure Dale, Freda, Bert, Clarisa, Angela, and Emily were there too, along with The Sleuths. It wouldn't be too difficult—it was the only nice place in town to eat.

CHAPTER 7

INVITATION TO A MISS MARPLE-ING

I DROPPED Agatha off at home before driving to the Airbnb the hens were staying at. Convincing the hens—Mabel, Bernice, and Doris—to eat dinner was the equivalent of announcing they'd won the gossip-fest lottery.

After the hen party, I headed back into town to visit the one and only hotel, off the town square, most definitely a step up in price and amenities.

Angela and Clarisa were a different story, especially since I began my conversation by asking for the hen's refunds on the Veronica Steele tickets.

"Absolutely not," Clarisa shot as she peered through the foot-wide crack she'd opened the door.

I knew better than to quote library code to Clarisa—she'd just quote it back.

I backed up and turned to leave, telling myself I could take the funds out of The Maplewood Public Library. No. No. I always gave in and did what other people expected me to do. *Be the doormat. Don't raise too much fuss. Don't ask for anything that requires anyone to be uncomfortable.* A residual survival mode from being raised in foster care. Well, I was done.

James was sitting in jail and planning to go to prison for something he didn't do. My new friends, the hens, had spent their bank accounts to come to something they should have enjoyed for free. And they didn't enjoy it because they didn't like Veronica. They were gaslighted into it.

I turned back to the hotel room and stuck my foot in the door before Clarisa could close it.

"Whaaa…"

"If you feel more comfortable talking in the lobby, join me there, but I need to talk to Angela."

Clarisa may be her best friend, but she didn't run the library.

"She's not here. She went to the bank."

Why would she go to Maplewood Credit Union? We didn't have any large banks here. For that we had to drive to Grandview.

"She went back to Grandview?"

"Yes," she whispered. She grabbed my elbow and pulled me in the room.

She plopped down in the marigold velvet chair, nearly disappearing against the fabric — her tailored suit the same bold golden shade. "Angela would kill me…sorry…bad choice of words…for telling you this."

I sat down in the matching chair and waited.

"Grandview Public Library has been having some financial problems."

It was my turn to be shocked. "What?"

"Yes, even with the ticket sales for Veronica's reading, we… I mean Angela, can't seem to make up the difference."

"The difference for what?"

"Me."

"What do you mean 'you'?"

"I may have taken some funds and invested them in bitcoin."

"And it didn't work out?"

"Worse. I lost money. Why do you think I'm at Angela's beck and call? Sure, we were coworkers, but not really friends."

I placed a hand on her arm. "I'm so sorry."

She glanced at my hand. "Yes, and this suit, not me at all. I mean look at me. I look like a pumpkin."

"So you're basically waiting on her hand and foot so she doesn't report you."

"You know what…" She paused and grabbed her purse from the dresser and then stood. "I'm turning myself in."

Something was still off. "How much did you lose?"

"A thousand dollars."

Sure, a thousand dollars is a loss for a large library like Grandview, but not enough to do what Angela was doing. Grandview had an outreach budget of at least a million dollars. Like I said, something was off.

"No, you are not," I said. "At least not yet."

Angela had to be the one responsible for the bulk of the missing funds and she was pinning the guilt on Clarisa.

"Change your clothes into something you like and come to dinner with us at The Tasty Burger. After my date with Detective Brandon, you can talk to him."

She relaxed. "Thank you, Gabby."

I waited in the hallway for her to change. I wasn't sure what I was going to say to Brandon about my showing up to our date with Grandview's assistant librarian. Then it came to me. I hadn't invited the other Sleuths yet.

I texted Emory, assuming Randolph was with him.

> Can you and Randolph come to dinner at The Tasty Burger at 5:30?

Emory texted back immediately.

> We'll be there. You're not going to believe what the autopsy showed.

Leave it to Emory to break the rules and give me (and The Sleuths) official information before Detective Brandon. I loved him for it. Okay, liked a lot. I had to be careful how I responded because he still had a crush on me.

I texted back:

> What did you and Randolph learn?

The dots played across the screen forever. Then his message popped up.

> You're not going to believe this… I mean, obviously you will because you're smart and brilliant and all that… but still—HUGE.

More dots. He was really dragging this out.

> Veronica had a brain tumor. Frontal lobe. Big one. Glioblastoma. That's the kind that messes with your head—literally. Mood swings, paranoia, totally explains why she was acting like… well… Veronica. It's classic tumor behavior.

More dots.

> Point is, she was dying anyway. Tumor like that? She wouldn't have made it six months. Which means… someone got real impatient.

I stared at the screen, connecting the dots faster than Emory could type them. Miss Marple always said when people act out of character, there's usually a reason—and it's rarely a good one. A tumor pressing on Veronica's brain? That explained the mood swings, the paranoia… even rewriting her will like a woman trying to settle unfinished business before the clock ran out.

Clarisa opened the door. She sported trendy jeans that didn't bunch at the ankles. Instead, they accented her muscular legs. She had changed into pink boots and a pink sweater with a giant daisy on the front. She adjusted her sweater. "This is so much better."

"Mind if we go to my house so I can change and take Agatha out?"

"Why do you need to change? I love your plaid pants. Where do you shop?"

I glanced down at my brown plaid pants. "Second Hand Chic."

"Is that in Maplewood?"

"Yes, next to Clearview Realty Group, across the street from the library."

"I'm going to have to stop there before we leave town."

"I can drop you there and pick you up on the way to The Tasty Burger."

She squeezed her hands together and squealed. "Oh, could you!"

Who was this? This was the real Clarisa—not the robotic, guilt-ridden servant Angela had molded.

While her hands were clasped, I couldn't help but notice her defined biceps. Ignoring social etiquette in favor of unfiltered curiosity, I blurted, "Do you lift?"

"Yes," she said, matter-of-factly. "I'm a triathlete."

So the suits Angela insisted Clarisa wore were more than trying to clone herself. They were to hide the powerful woman, literally, beneath. The badly fitting suits made Clarisa feel frumpy, dominated, and weak.

The drive was less than half a mile.

As she hopped out, Clarisa smiled. "I could've walked."

"Small town perks," I said, returning the smile. "I'll grab you at five-fifteen?"

She nodded and started to close the door, but I stopped her. "Clarisa?"

"Yeah?"

"Do you think Angela would kill to protect her reputation?"

Clarisa hesitated for half a breath. "She'd do anything."

CHAPTER 8
WRESTLE MANIA AT THE TASTY BURGER

I PICKED up Clarisa early enough to arrive early at The Tasty Burger to set the stage for my plan.

In Miss Marple novels, she sat knitting in the corner while the suspects incriminated themselves in hotel lobbies, restaurants, or her own living room. This wasn't a novel, so I'd have to set the stage myself.

I planned to sit in the middle of the restaurant with Brandon and arrange the rest of the suspects around us.

The hens arrived first, clucking about the atmosphere and how much The Tasty Burger reminded them of a restaurant they'd frequented as teens in the fifties.

Bernice shouldered her large bag with knitting needles poking out. "Thank you for inviting us. Who would have thought this would turn into a real murder-mystery weekend?"

"Someone really died, Bernice," Mabel chided as she slid out a chair for her and practically shoved her into it.

"That woman was venomous..."

"It's just horrid," Doris interrupted. "But so exciting."

I was hoping Bernice was about to spill some vital information, but before I could ask her to finish her thought, Freda and Bert arrived.

Freda slung her oversized handbag onto the table I led them to.

"Exactly why are we here?" Bert asked, eyeing me like I'd dragged him into a trap.

"She's Miss Marpling us—or whatever you call it." Freda dug into her cavernous bag and produced a tangle of recording equipment. With a flourish, she slammed a mic down on the table. "I'm going to record."

I froze. Was I that predictable? What did I say? She was right but I didn't want the rest of the guests to know what was going on. I opened my mouth to say something but nothing came out.

"You think we killed Veronica?" Bert asked. He hadn't sat down yet. Hands on his hips, he looked undecided about whether to commit to the chair or to throttle me in defense of his girlfriend.

"Oh, sit down, Bert." She pushed record. "Hey listeners, it's Freda... and this is True Crime Lovers. Normally, this is where I'd tell you about Veronica Steele's latest book or wildest plot twist, but tonight... it's real. Veronica's gone. I can't believe I'm saying that. But I promised—this podcast would always follow her stories... and now, I have to follow the biggest one of all. Who killed Veronica Steele?"

I stood transfixed and prayed she didn't ask me a question.

The door opened and The Sleuths arrived, saving me. Thomas, ever the former councilman, led the way, followed by Randolph and Emory, deep in conversation, Antonio bringing up the rear.

I pointed to the table on the left of mine and Brandon's.

"Where is Agatha?" Antonio asked.

"I left her at home tonight."

He scanned the room, looking for Brandon I'm sure.

"Is this a date?"

Emory paused and looked me full in the face. The familiar flush of teenage crush crept up his neck, even though he wasn't a teen.

I swallowed hard and averted my gaze from Emory. "Yes, Detective Brandon is coming for a date."

"Crowded for a date." Antonio slapped his doughy hands together. "I know. This is your engagement party."

Ever since I'd proposed to Brandon under the influence of a few sips of wine, Antonio was like Agatha with a bone. He wouldn't let it go. He'd hound us until we actually tied the knot, which at this pace would be…well…never.

Clarisa had seated herself at a table with her eyes on the door, waiting for Angela. Angela arrived wearing her signature pants suit. Her mouth fell open when she spied Clarisa in her daisy sweater and trendy jeans. She didn't acknowledge anyone. Instead, she marched to Clarisa's table.

No "hello." No "how are you, friend?"

"I thought we had an agreement."

"You had an agreement." Clarisa plopped the cup of water she'd been drinking down on the table and it sloshed out, making a large puddle, which turned into a trickle over the side of the table. I grabbed a handful of napkins from the dispenser at The Sleuths table and ran to sop it up.

Angela ignored me and the water dripped onto the floor. "I can turn you in to the authorities."

"No need. I'm turning myself in."

I squeezed the napkin over the glass releasing the water. Instead of hearing a pin drop, it was the tinkle of water.

The moment didn't last. Freda appeared with her mic.

"Folks, I think we may have a confession here." Freda set the mic on the freshly wiped table, eyes blazing at Clarisa. If looks could kill, Clarisa would've been toast.

Freda clicked off the recorder and lunged, grabbing for Clarisa's neck. "You murdered Veronica!"

But Freda's enthusiasm outweighed her skill. Clarisa, all bulky muscle under her daisy-patterned sweater and ripped jeans, twisted free like it was second nature.

One sharp pivot and a sweep of the leg sent Freda sprawling onto the floor, flat on her back with a stunned "*oof.*"

Clarisa stood over her, barely winded. "I didn't kill Veronica," she snapped, voice steady but tight. "I lost the money. All of it. The library funds I—stupidly— skimmed off? Gone. Some scam promising Bitcoin profits." She shook her head, disgusted. "Turns out, I'm better at triathlons than crypto."

The room fell into an awkward, stunned silence, all eyes darting between them.

Clarisa straightened, tugging her daisy sweater back into place. "Next time, maybe lead with questions…not chokeholds."

Freda lay on the floor a few seconds longer, her hands over her face, sobbing quietly. Bert must have joined the scene in the middle of the wrestling match. He hadn't intervened. Now he sunk down on the floor next to Freda.

"I'm sorry honey."

I needed to get this mess cleaned up and reset the stage before Detective Brandon arrived.

As if right on cue, he stepped through the door and took in the scene: Freda still sobbing on the floor, Bert's arms wrapped around her, Clarisa pacing with adrenaline still buzzing through her, and Angela—usually unflappable—slumped in her seat, looking completely defeated.

I ran to him. "It's okay, Brandon. Everything is under control."

"You missed the wrestle mania," Bernice cooed, her knitting needles clacking away.

Clarisa stopped. "Detective, may I…" she paused to glare at Angela, "speak to you privately?"

My plan was circling the drain. Forget circling. It had plunked down the pipe, forced by the drano of the scene that just transpired.

"Yes, Clarisa, but I'd like to talk to Gabby for a minute."

Brandon took me by the elbow and led me back to the hallway housing the public restrooms.

"I see what you're trying to do. Poirot the murder or something."

I was too upset to correct him, but my brain wasn't. Miss Marple it.

Instead I blurted out,"The best-laid plans of mice and men, you know…so often go awry."[1]

"So I'm right. You wanted to get the people *you think* are suspects in a room on our date.'

"I thought they'd talk. I didn't know they'd start wrestle mania," I answered, using Bernice's words.

He leaned back against the wall and crossed his arms. "Does Clarisa want to confess to murdering Veronica?"

"No. She took a thousand dollars from the Grandview Library funds and blew it on a bitcoin scam."

"Oh." He paused. "Is she dangerous?"

"No," I lied. Visions of her slamming Freda to the floor replayed in my mind. Then I thought better of it. "Unless you grab her around the neck in a chokehold."

"That's what happened?"

"Yes, Angela has had Clarisa in a virtual chokehold since the Bitcoin scam, making her a servant and convincing her she'd do hard time if Angela told the authorities—her words, not mine."

"She *could* do time."

"She knows that, but she's tired of being under Angela's thumb. She's ready to come clean."

He nodded and pushed off the wall.

"That's not all."

"What else is there?"

"Angela charged patrons for tickets to see Veronica. Those hens… Doris, Bernice, and Mabel, drained their bank accounts to come here."

"And what does that have to do with the murder investigation?"

"Nothing really. It just bugs me. Angela is all superior about it. Do you know what she said to me?" I paused, took a deep breath, straightened to mimic Angela's hoity posture, and continued, "'The tickets are perfectly legal, Gabrielle. West Virginia Code 10-1-9A. Libraries are permitted to establish reasonable fees for programs deemed beneficial to the community.'"

"She really gets under your skin, doesn't she?" He chuckled.

I didn't think the situation was funny. It was serious. But if I was honest, it was the other comment that stuck me in my pride.

"'I'm sure your… modest branch will catch up to Grandview's standards one day.'"

I must have said it aloud because Brandon replied, "I'm sorry for laughing." He pulled me toward him. "She's just noise. Your library is top-notch. You know that."

I murmured into his chest—it wasn't sweet nothings, but it was all I had right now. "Except my library's a microcosm for murder… and our star author, James, is suspect number one."

He released me and looked me full in the face, brushing a strand of hair out of my eye. "Let me handle the investigation. I'll make sure if James is innocent, he gets cleared."

I bit my tongue at the word *if*.

"Why don't you sleuth out this Angela character instead? Don't they have library police or something?"

I snorted. "Library police? Sadly, no badges or flashing lights. But… the State Library Commission oversees all that budget and compliance nonsense. If Angela's skimming off the top, they'll find it."

Brandon's mouth curved. "Good. Let's keep you sleuthing financial reports, not murder suspects."

"You're a genius, Brandon." I leaned forward and planted a quick kiss on his lips. "I'm going to contact the State Library Commission—"

I didn't get the opportunity to finish that sentence because he pulled me close, kissing me long and hard, effectively shutting down my train of thought.

We barely noticed we'd drifted out of the hallway into the main dining room until—

"They did it—they got engaged! Can I see the ring?" Antonio's voice boomed across the restaurant.

Brandon and I stumbled forward, red-faced, only to find the entire diner staring at us.

The hens clapped like schoolgirls at a sock hop, Bernice's knitting needles clicking in applause.

Emory, though, wasn't clapping. He sat frozen, a flush creeping up his neck. His eyes flicked from Brandon to me, full of something he couldn't quite hide.

Bernice leaned over to Doris and whispered much too loudly, "Poor Emory. He thought she'd pick him."

Doris swatted her with a french fry. "Hush, you'll make it worse."

But Emory had already ducked his head, pretending to study the menu like it held the answers to life, love, and murder.

The restaurant erupted in laughter.

While Brandon and I basked in the pure chaos created by the misinformation Antonio had unleashed, I couldn't help but laugh as Clarisa launched herself at me, nearly knocking me back with a full-blown bear hug.

"Careful," Brandon warned, grinning. "She's fragile."

Clarisa ignored him, still squeezing the life out of me. "Thank you," she whispered fiercely. "For not letting Angela railroad me."

Brandon gently peeled her off me. "Okay, hero, save it for tomorrow. Come by the station in the morning. We'll get your statement sorted."

The laughter and teasing continued around us, congratulations echoing through The Tasty Burger as Brandon laced his fingers through mine.

Brandon leaned close, his jaw tight and his voice pitched low enough for only me. "We need to clear this up before Antonio starts planning a wedding menu. Let's get out of here and finish this date somewhere without a built-in audience."

We were halfway to the door, practically home free, when the glass swung open with a jingle—and in blew the storm.

Brittany—reporter, professional pot-stirrer, and possibly allergic to timing—stormed in, phone in hand, face smug enough to clear the room of oxygen.

"Hope I'm not too late," she called, holding up her phone like a trophy. "Article's live."

The room stilled.

Brandon's hand tightened around mine. "Gabby,"

he muttered, warning stitched into his tone, but I was already bracing for impact.

Brittany cleared her throat with dramatic flair. "In case anyone missed the breaking news—James settled out of court with Veronica years ago. Over that little… manuscript theft incident." She arched a brow, clearly enjoying herself. "Big settlement. Bigger scandal. But poor James? She painted him as the villain."

Murmurs rippled through the restaurant like wildfire.

"And here's the kicker," Brittany continued, grinning as she twisted the knife. "James is the beneficiary of half of Veronica's estate."

My stomach dropped. *The will?* How did Brittany know about that? I was certain Dale had told me in confidence—and I hadn't told anyone. I risked a glance at him, but his reaction offered no comfort. His brow furrowed, the faintest frown creasing between his eyes, and then he turned that look on me. Not accusatory exactly, but enough to make my pulse stutter. A warning. A question. Maybe even the hint of an *I told you so.*

The room erupted—gasps, accusations, the hens practically fainting into their milkshakes.

Brandon's jaw flexed. "So much for a quiet exit."

I exhaled through my nose, fire crackling low in my chest. The evening had officially derailed, but one thing was certain:

This wasn't over

Freda shot to her feet, clutching her mic like it might capture the chaos. Her eyes darted wildly, as if hunting for the perfect line to open her next podcast episode.

Bert lumbered up after her, not frantic but fuming,

his jaw clenched tight. He swiped a hand down his face and muttered a curse under his breath that made the hens gasp louder than Brittany's headline.

The hens clucked and gasped, their voices tangling together in a rising pitch, outrage and excitement indistinguishable.

And then came Emily, Veronica's protégé, slipping in behind Brittany. Her face was drained of color, but her eyes—sharp and wet—burned with something raw and unguarded. Not outrage. Not grief. Something smaller. Childlike. Bewilderment. Confusion.

"We're leaving," Brandon muttered, steering me toward the door as accusations flew, Freda's voice rose sharp and frantic, the hens clucked in a flurry of gasps, and Emily's wide-eyed stare burned through me. My thoughts tumbled over themselves—James and the estate, Clarisa's confession, Angela's schemes. Everything was unraveling faster than I could stitch it together.

And somehow, I knew… the worst was still waiting to show its face.

CHAPTER 9
SIGNED, SEALED...
SUSPECT

EVERY PUFF of romance evaporated into the crisp autumn air. The same breathlessness I'd felt from the kiss shifted into a fresh anxiousness for James. The date ended in the parking lot.

"Hey, you're leaving?" Brittany yelled from the side exit that was reserved for emergencies.

"Yes, I'm going to have some extra work to do because of your article and I'd like to know where you got the information about Veronica's will," Brandon responded.

"I wasn't talking to you..." Brittany said with one hand on her hip.

Someone yelled a muffled command from inside The Tasty Burger.

"Oh relax, it's just me," she called, tossing her hair over one shoulder. "I come in this way all the time. The staff know me."

As if in response to her declaration, a polite but

unmistakable beep began somewhere inside the building.

One beep.

Two.

Three.

Then all at once, the alarm blared like a fire truck caught in a megaphone, bouncing off the alley walls.

Brandon's phone buzzed at his hip. He sighed before he even read the alert. "The Tasty Burger."

"I'm not breaking in," Brittany shouted over the din, hands over her ears. "I'm *exiting with confidence.*"

"Confidence doesn't override the security system," he said, already tapping on his screen.

"I've been in and out of this door for years. This has never happened."

"Then congratulations. You've finally overstayed your welcome," Brandon replied, grimly.

I swallowed hard, heat prickling at the back of my neck.

The alarm finally cut off, leaving an echoing silence and a faint buzzing in my ears. Brittany fluffed her hair back into place as if nothing had happened.

"Well, *that* was rude," she huffed. "You'd think a town burger joint could tell the difference between me and an intruder."

"They can," Brandon said, sliding his phone back into his coat. "That's why it went off."

Brandon turned from me and opened his SUV door. "I'll see you tomorrow."

"Gabby, don't leave. Let me grab my take-out order and I'll fill you in."

Brandon paused, his hands on the steering wheel,

the overhead light giving his hair an angelic glow—
well, scratch that—after he turned and I saw his expression, it was more like a creature whose den had just
been disturbed.

Miss Marple would've called it at once: not anger,
but indignation. The kind that comes when someone's
sense of justice has been poked one too many times by
someone with no sense of boundaries. And if there was
one thing more dangerous than a cornered suspect, it
was a man like Brandon Hale—measured, methodical—
who'd just decided he no longer had patience for polite
diplomacy.

He slid a leg out and then the other in a slow deliberate motion. Once he had both feet on the ground, he
spread them and crossed his arms.

"I think you've told all to the whole restaurant."

"And the internet," I added, trying to support Brandon, but also be a mediator for both of them.

Brittany adjusted her leather satchel and clapped her
hands together. "I know! It's hit the big time. It's
syndicated."

I froze, glancing back and forth between them like a
spectator at a tennis match. Brittany's expression
remained bright and unfazed, practically glowing with
enthusiasm. Brandon, on the other hand, looked like he
was about to blow a gasket. He exhaled sharply, and the
cold air puffed into a frosty cloud around his head—just
enough to make it look like steam really *was* coming out
of his ears, exactly as I'd imagined.

"Yeah," Brittany continued, oblivious to Brandon's
huffing. "I'm getting calls and texts to be on podcasts,
including Freda's." She held up her phone as proof with

what I assumed was a text from Freda. "A few national shows want me on." She turned and grabbed my elbows and jumped up and down. "Gabby, this is it. This is my big break!"

How did I support my boyfriend, my best friend, and James, who was another best friend?

Gabby's big break was always more important than anyone or anything. Everyone was supposed to understand this and not only acknowledge it, but cheer her on, no matter how it affected…well…me, and other people.

She'd gotten her job with the Grandview Gazette and that was her big break.

Brandon uncrossed his arms and set one foot on the edge of his vehicle. "While you're enjoying your big break, I have to go deal with the consequences." He slid into the driver's seat, slammed the door, hit the start button, dropped it into gear, and peeled out of the parking lot.

"Gosh, you'd think he'd be happy I put this town on the map."

I turned toward her and squinted, scrunching up my face in full Miss Marple mode—the sort of look that wasn't so much judgmental as "I see more than I'm letting on."

"You're wrinkling up your face like Miss Marple," Brittany said, one hand flying to her hip. "What did I do wrong *this* time?"

"James." That was all I said.

Her hand dropped. Her face fell with it. "I don't make the news, Gabby. I just write it. You know that."

I took a slow breath. "I do. I really do. And I know

your job matters—telling the truth, asking questions that make people uncomfortable when they need to be." I glanced toward the parking lot where Brandon's vehicle had been parked. He was already juggling damage control. "But he's walking into this storm, and right now you've got the biggest umbrella."

Any chance of getting James off the hook for murder had just been blown out of the water, regardless of what the forensic evidence said. The story she'd gone viral with would stain James's reputation in the community —and possibly sink him at trial.

She opened her mouth, then closed it again.

"But maybe there's a chance you can do more with your big break," I added, voice softening. " You could help James. Hercule Poirot once said, *'It is always the facts that will not fit in that are significant.'*"

Brittany blinked, the quote catching her mid-defensive breath.

"You've got a gift for finding the pieces that don't quite fit," I said. "The details people miss. Maybe your interviews, your research—they could help clear James's name before he ends up on death row."

Brittany tilted her head, as if I'd just handed her a camera lens she hadn't thought to try.

"You can use your voice to help this time," I finished, offering a small smile. "Miss Marple would."

Her face lit up with an epiphany. "Let's do it," she said.

"What?"

"Let's go through all my interviews and files and you find what I missed. I mean it is sweet of you to say I find, what was it? 'the facts that don't fit in,' but that's all you. I just report the facts that slap me in the face."

I agreed, not with words, but with a slight nod. Because her concession was only partly true. She shared the facts that would slap people like a wet fish when they opened the news app.

She placed her hand on the emergency exit door. "Let me get my food."

"Why don't you use the front door this time?"

She paused, hand slipping from the handle. "Don't you want to see Detective Handsome Pants again?" She wiggled her brows. "He's got that whole brooding Poirot energy going—*Death on the Nile* style. All that's missing is the mustache and a murder aboard a steamer."

"Not in the state that he is in right now." I didn't add the fact he was in the state because of her. I knew her—she had a good heart, but... she needed grace for her lack of relational intelligence.

"I need to go home and walk Agatha. Meet me there?"

She trotted to the front of The Tasty Burger and yelled over her shoulder. "I'll grab you and Agatha some food too."

It was then I realized I hadn't eaten.

There was no reason to yell or text her my order. It never changed. Neither did Agatha's. As I crossed the lot to my car, the cold nipped at my cheeks, and I could almost hear the din of conversation spilling out from The Tasty Burger. Today's special: *"Did James really do it?"* with a generous side of *"When is the engagement party?"*

No doubt Antonio was inside, sitting at his usual booth with that wide-eyed certainty only he could pull off. In his mind, the hallway kiss between Brandon and me was as binding as a courthouse wedding. I could practically hear him now: *"Miss Gabby, if he kissed you like that, doesn't that mean you're engaged? That's how it works in the movies."*

Thomas, ever the realist, would try to explain. Something about context. Timing. Intent. But Antonio would just shake his head, unconvinced. Romance, to him, was simple math. One kiss + one hallway = one lifetime commitment.

I opened my car door, the corners of my mouth tugging into a reluctant smile.

If only things were that simple, Antonio. If only.

CHAPTER 10
FRONT YARD CONFESSIONS

AFTER FINDING the front door unlocked, I slipped inside and flipped on the lights. Maybe I'd forgotten to lock it… but the thought unsettled me.Agatha bounded out of her comfy bed, sniffing at me and my messenger bag for food. Finding none, she went back to her bed and curled up, keeping her sad brown eyes honed in on me as if to say – how could you not bring me a burger and fries?

"Come on, girl. You still need to go out and pee." I grabbed her harness and leash. She didn't budge. I squatted down and wrestled it on her little uncooperative dead-fish-like stance. "Don't worry. Aunt Brittany is bringing your food from The Tasty Burger."

At this statement, she sprung up, and shot to the door, the lead trailing behind her. I caught up with her and grabbed the leash end. I opened the door and she scrambled out onto the porch.

I joined her on the porch where she was sniffing the

concrete as if Brittany would have buried her burger and fries there.

"Hope you don't mind that I followed you home," a male voice said from the yard. One lone street lamp bounced off his fedora, making it look like he belonged in a 1930s crime novel.

He stepped further into the light.

"Dale, what are you doing here?"

Agatha leapt off the porch and joined him in the yard, taking the time to squat and pee before she licked his shoes. I maintained my safe distance by staying on the bottom step while Agatha pulled at her harness, willing me to join them in the middle of the yard.

"Why don't you tell me what you are doing here?" I asked again, the fear rising like bile in my throat. This wasn't the first time I'd been alone with a murder suspect. Maybe he came here tonight to kill me.

"I wanted to talk to you about Veronica."

I pulled Agatha closer, reeling her in on her leash like a fish. He'd already told me about her erratic spending and the new will, which he must have told Brittany about. Maybe he knew the *why* behind her behavior.

He stepped closer and I leaned over and picked up Agatha, holding her against my chest. Praying Miranda, my neighbor would come out her front door to chat. Or Brittany would pull up with our food.

"About her brain tumor?"

He reeled backward, catching himself on the maple tree and slipping in the wet leaves I should have raked up last week. "What?"

I opened the door and dropped Agatha in, clicking the lead off her harness. "You didn't know?"

"I think I need a drink of water," he said, leaning against the tree. "Oh Veronica, my dear. I didn't know. Why didn't you tell me?"

What did I do? Leave him to pass out in a gunky mushy pile of leaves? Invite him in, only to have him murder me? Or stand here awkwardly while he talked to his dead wife? I chose option three for about three seconds until he began a guttural sob.

"I'm sorry. I shouldn't have… you would still be here if I hadn't…"

Was that a confession? I'd left my phone inside. Brittany was taking forever to get here. What was the holdup? I spied a small pebble on the steps. I leaned over and picked it up, hoping I could hit Miranda's side window with it. She could call the police. Dale could confess to them.

It was clear to me now. Upset that his wife was bankrupting them, he poisoned her. He didn't know she had a brain tumor. Now hit with the information she was dying anyway, he had remorse. She couldn't have spent their whole fortune before she died, he probably reasoned with himself.

I threw the pebble against Miranda's kitchen window and it made the faintest whisper of a ping before hitting the ground. Fail. She wouldn't have heard it if she had music on or was running water at the sink.

I sat on the steps, ready to bolt inside if Dale moved. He continued to sob and utter incoherent phrases. "If only you would have told me… I wouldn't have…"

It was then I remembered his request for water. "Dale, will you be okay if I get you a glass of water?"

"And some tissues please."

I stumbled inside and zipped to the kitchen. I pulled a glass out of the cabinet and filled it with filtered water from the fridge, grabbing my phone, pushing record, all before shoving a box of tissues under my arm.

When I stepped back out on the porch and looked over to the maple, he was gone. I sat down hard on the wicker chair to my left and bounded back up quicker than squirrel Agatha liked to chase up a tree. Someone was already sitting in the chair.

"Sorry to scare you Gabby, but that wet pile of leaves is stinky and not comfortable at all."

I handed him the water and the tissues before taking the wicker chair on the other side of the door. What could I do? Run back inside and slam the door on his face. I'm sure that's what most sane people would do. But not mystery lovers like me. Not friends of the accused who didn't murder Veronica. Sure, I could sit on the porch with a murderer, get a full confession on my phone and then end up dead, buried under a rotting pile of leaves in my front yard.

He chugged the water before blowing his nose.

"How do you know she had a brain tumor?"

No. I'm supposed to be the one asking the questions here. Or I just knit like Bernice or Miss Marple and you talk. I listen, then figure out the "how you did it."

"I'm kind of friends with the coroner." By that, I meant the young coroner had a crush on me and is in a group called The Sleuths and we solve murders in our spare time.

"Oh, I didn't think they released that kind of…" he choked and took another sip of water, "personal information to the public."

"Oh, they don't." If they did, Brittany would have written it in her article.

I waited for him to say something.

"I'm in shock. I mean it makes sense. Her erratic behavior…"

He set the glass down on the porch floor and blew his nose again. I thought of what Emory had said about the tumor.

"Yes, the coroner said it could cause mood swings and paranoia."

"If I could have just waited and not acted…" He blew his nose again.

Was he about to confess? For the second time?

Agatha put her paws on the glass storm door and let out a few complaining yaps. *Where is my food you promised?*

Dale jerked his head in her direction. "Cute dog." Then he turned and grabbed another tissue.

"What am I going to do Gabby? I have to tell someone or I'm going to die, or explode from guilt." He raised both hands in the air and waved the tissue like a flag of surrender.

This was it. He was going to confess.

The blare of the siren overrode whatever he said next. Miranda stepped out on her porch and flipped her security lights on, lighting up the block like an after hours block party. Brandon's police SUV screeched to a stop in front of my house as if I were a kidnap victim, not a librarian sitting on her front porch waiting for a murderer to confess.

"Did you call the police?" He dropped his wad of tissues and knocked the empty glass of water over when he stood to his full six foot two frame. The glass rolled off the porch and shattered on the sidewalk.

He shook a fist at me and I cowered away from him.

"I wanted to tell you everything and now you've ruined it."

A swat team pulled up in an olive green van. Officers Greg and Shane hopped out.

Brandon held a megaphone up to his mouth which was totally overkill. "Dale, come out with your hands up."

First of all, he was already out. Secondly, we could hear him without the megaphone. Greg and Shane breached the yard and slipped in the sloppy pile of rotting maple leaves. Greg caught himself on the branch of the tree before going down on one knee and aiming a weapon at me.

"Pretty sure you're not supposed to aim that at me."

"Sorry, Gabby."

Dales' shoulders slumped forward. The anger and frustration of a moment ago were gone. "No need for weapons. I'll come willingly."

Then he turned back to me. "I was going to tell you everything. I thought you could help me."

"I'm sorry," I mouthed.

A bright light flashed in our faces and I looked down to see Brittany crouching on the sidewalk, on the broken glass.

"I heard it on the police scanner," she said as she

took photos of Greg and Shane leading Dale away in handcuffs. "I parked around the back in the alley."

She stood and blood oozed out of a hole in jeans where a shard of glass stood at attention in her knee.

"You're bleeding." I jerked her up on the porch by grabbing her wrist.

The swat team, consisting of Greg and Shane, left as well as Detective Brandon, who hadn't even waved or said "thank you."

"I've got a first aid kit," Miranda yelled from her front porch. "Be right over."

I grabbed the food from Brittany's Red Supersonic Toyota 4Runner while Miranda removed the glass and cleaned the wound.

"Wounded in the line of duty," Brittany joked. "I'm adding that to my next article."

"How about your friend who sat outside with a murderer and talked him down," Miranda said as she gave the wound an extra spray of hydrogen peroxide.

"Ouch."

"Is that little bitty scratch hurting you?" Miranda continued.

She turned to me. "I saw him out there sobbing in the leaf pile. He was losing it."

"So you got my signal?"

"What signal?"

"Nevermind." So the pebble on the window hadn't worked.

"When he moved to the porch when you were inside, I called the police."

"Durn it."

"I think this is the part where you say 'thank you,'"

Miranda pulled the sleeves down on her satin robe and then packed up the first aid kit.

"Thank you, but…"

"But what? If you keep inviting murderer suspects over, I'm going to have to use my own real estate service to find another neighborhood."

I crossed my arms. "I never invite them here. They just come."

Miranda smacked me on the shoulder. "I'm just kidding. I mean, what would we talk about at the office if we didn't have you Miss Marpling our town?"

"I'm going to pee," Brittany said as she hobbled out of the kitchen.

"He was about to confess."

Brittany did a one-eighty on one foot.

"Confess to what?"

"Murdering his wife."

"Wait, what?" Brittany and Miranda gasped in stereo.

"I think we need some coffee before we hear the whole story."

Agatha ate her fries and small burger with joyful snarling sounds. Brittany plated our food and we shared with Miranda, who picked at the fries. I loaded the coffee filter and set it to brew. By the time we'd poured our first cup of coffee, I felt ready and full enough to share the whole ordeal.

By the time the salty-sweet scent of fries settled into the corners of my kitchen, the three of us had carved out our usual places—me at the counter, Brittany perched on the stool with one leg outstretched like a wounded war hero, and Miranda swirling her coffee like it was wine and she was at a tasting event rather than sitting in a librarian's kitchen after midnight with ketchup on her sleeve.

"So," Brittany prompted. "Start from the beginning. And don't skip any of the weird parts."

I took a long sip. "He was already in my yard when I got home."

"Creepy," Miranda muttered, dabbing fry grease off her fingers with a napkin.

"He said he wanted to talk about Veronica. Then when I mentioned the brain tumor—he didn't know."

Brittany's eyebrows shot up. "Wait. What brain tumor? He went on and on about her spending and her new will when I spoke to him earlier. Like she was bankrupting *him*."

So she did talk to Dale. It made sense that he would want the world to know that James was the beneficiary of half of Veronica's estate. He created his own misdirect using Brittany's article.

"Exactly. He looked like someone hit him with a leaf rake." I paused, picturing his stunned face beneath that fedora, lit by one pathetic streetlamp and the unspoken truth. "That's when he started losing it. Talking to her like she was still here. Crying in the leaf pile. I thought it was going to be a full confession."

"But then…" Brittany prompted, gesturing dramatically with her half-eaten burger.

"Then you showed up with the cavalry and a flashlight in my eyeball," I said.

"Excuse me for bleeding on the scene," Brittany said, holding up her gauze-wrapped knee like a badge of honor.

"I wasn't sure what to do," I admitted. "He was on the edge, but I didn't want him to bolt. Or worse."

"I'm glad Miranda called the police," Brittany said. "Even if her porch robe makes her look like a glamorous soap opera villain."

"Thank you," Miranda said with a prim smile. "It's vintage satin."

"He was about to say something important right before the sirens," I said. "I just don't know what. Something about regret. About acting too soon."

Miranda frowned. "Too soon?"

"He said if he'd known about the tumor, he wouldn't have done it. Wouldn't have… something."

Brittany's pen was already out, scribbling notes on a receipt. "I need quotes. And a title. How about *Tears and Tissues: A Porchside Confession?*"

"You are so weird," I said fondly, handing her the last fry.

Miranda leaned back in her chair. "You think he really did it? Killed her?"

"I think so. It was poison, after all. And maybe he didn't mean to kill her right then, but if he gave it to her knowing what it could do… that's still murder."

We sat for a moment in silence, the air humming with caffeine and something heavier.

Agatha snored softly from her bed, belly full, the only one in the house truly at peace.

"Gabby," Brittany said, "you might've just solved this thing."

"Maybe," I said, tapping the side of my mug. "But he didn't finish the story. And murderers? They always leave something out."

CHAPTER 11
PLAGIARIZED PAGES AND POWDERED SUGAR

THE LIBRARY HAD BEEN CLEARED to open, but Maplewood wasn't exactly rushing through the doors. Who wanted to step inside the same building where a murder had happened—and where the newspaper had already crowned James the killer?

Our own literary hero, the man this town once bragged about like a prize ribbon, knocked clean off his throne with one ugly headline. James wasn't a murderer. I knew it. But the town gobbled up every printed word and turned their backs on him anyway. After everything he'd given them, this was their thanks?

The story hour kids and moms didn't show. Allison, their appointed leader, shot me a text.

Sorry, Gabby. We can't come until this whole murder business is cleared up.

I texted back.

I understand.

She replied with,

Poor James

If that's what it would take to get them back, I'd do it.

While I hoped Dale had confessed to Detective Brandon and this whole murder business was cleaned up, I hadn't heard from him. I'd made Brittany promise not to turn in her article *Tears and Tissues: A Porchside Confession*, regarding Dale's confession last night, until I heard from Brandon.

And true to form, he had not called or texted me last night or this morning. It was as if he was afraid I would share pertinent information with The Sleuths at our meeting this morning. Which, to be honest, I would. But that didn't mean he couldn't send me a text to say "goodnight" or "great kiss in the hallway." My face flushed when I thought about the kiss. I slapped my face with both hands.

My first order of business was the Grandview Library fiasco. I drafted an email to the State Library Commission, outlining Angela's little pay-to-enter scheme at Veronica Steele's reading—and, while I was at it, the not-so-little matter of misappropriated funds.

Subject: Formal Concern Regarding Grandview Library and Ms. Angela Hartwell
Dear Members of the State Library Commission,
I'm writing to formally report a concern involving Angela

Hartwell of Grandview Library. She charged patrons for Veronica Steele's author reading held at our public library without prior approval. Additionally, there are troubling signs of potential fund misappropriation at Grandview. I respectfully request a review.
Thank you,
Gabby Keats
Head Librarian, Maplewood Public Library

I probably should have mentioned Clarisa but as far as I knew she was at the police station confessing. If the State Library Commission did a review, the missing one thousand dollars would come up. Not to mention the fact that I should have done some more investigating, but again, I'd leave that to the State Library Commission. I'd done what Brandon asked me to do. Now, with the new information…or, scratch that…Dale's near confession on my porch, I was ready to clear James's name so things could get back to normal around here.

I missed the kids this morning and hearing about their latest game or interest. I busied myself instead with firing up the coffee machine and making myself an espresso. My assistant, Mary, volunteered to go grab some donuts for The Sleuths.

Agatha yapped at the door with the urgency of someone late for a very important pastry appointment. Her paws clicked against the hardwood as she danced in place, glancing between Mary and the doorknob like she might open it herself if we took too long.

Mary shrugged on her light quilted jacket, one of those burnt-orange numbers that made her look like a walking pumpkin spice latte. "She wants to come."

"Oh, she *decided*, did she?" I said, watching Agatha's cinnamon-colored curls bounce with anticipation. "This isn't about fresh air. It's about sugar."

Agatha gave me a long, exaggerated blink. The look of a dog who knew exactly what she was doing and didn't care that I saw right through her.

She didn't need the walk—her little doggy legs got plenty of action chasing squirrels from our postage-stamp yard—but she *knew* Lottie at the bakery always had a paper napkin lined with powdered donut holes waiting for her. And somehow, no one in town questioned why a dog got VIP status at Maplewood's most popular bakery.

The crisp scent of fallen leaves and just-baked cinnamon bread wafted in as Mary opened the door. Agatha bolted outside like a sugar-fueled rocket, ears flapping, tail curled high.

"I should've named her Pavlov," I muttered.

The library door chimed its usual cheerful jingle, but the sound struck me sideways. I wasn't expecting anyone just yet—especially not *him*.

Owen stepped inside, letting the autumn breeze drift in behind him with a whisper of drying leaves and distant cinnamon. His shoulders hunched like he expected judgment to pounce from the nearest bookshelf.

I blinked. "Owen?"

He looked up, startled, as if he'd hoped to sneak in unnoticed. "Hey. Um. Hope I'm not too early?"

"You're not," I said slowly, marking my place in The Sleuths' folder with a Maplewood Public Library bookmark. "You're just… here. Which I didn't expect."

He nodded once, hands shoved in the pockets of his gray hoodie. He looked like he hadn't shaved since the reading. "I haven't exactly been reliable lately."

That was putting it gently. He hadn't returned texts, hadn't answered calls.

I folded my arms. "I thought maybe you were done with all this."

"I thought about it," he admitted. "But I can't be. Not when James is—Gabby, he didn't do it."

His voice caught slightly on the last word, and for a moment, the new Owen—the newly confident author, the man who'd finally found his voice—was gone, replaced by the Owen I knew— the college kid who used to shove donut holes into his briefcase and hope no one noticed he'd written his notes in color-coded symbols to keep the words from swimming.

"I believe that too," I said softly. "But the police aren't convinced."

He ran a hand through his curls and dropped onto a chair, letting out a breath that sounded like it had been trapped since the night of the reading.

"I feel like I should've spoken up. Said something when they started looking at him sideways. But I just stood there. And Veronica—" his voice faltered, "—she was praising me, Gabby. Going on about how my 'voice sparkled.' Meanwhile, James looked like he couldn't breathe."

I pulled up a chair beside him. "She wasn't just a sore subject for him. She was the reason he almost quit writing. Twenty years ago, Veronica stole his manuscript. Word for word. Passed it off as her debut. Nearly ended him."

Owen looked stunned. "He never told me that."

"He doesn't tell many people. He rebuilt his career from scratch. Mentored new writers—like you. And then she shows up here, acting like the Grande Dame of Crime Lit, and we're all supposed to pretend it's fine."

His jaw tightened. "It wasn't fine."

"No," I agreed. "But it's not too late to help him."

The doubt I'd tried to bury resurfaced. I'd told myself James and Owen would enjoy having a best-selling author at their library, that it would be a gift, a spark. But sitting here with Owen, I couldn't keep pretending. I hadn't brought them a gift. I'd brought Veronica—and all the damage she carried with her.

Outside, a leaf skittered past the window like a reminder: autumn waits for no one. Neither did grudges. Neither did regrets. And now, neither could I.

Owen met my eyes. "Tell me what I can do."

"I'll tell you what you can do. Stay here and help us. Brittany is coming to go over some files."

"What kind of files?"

"She did a bunch of research for the article she released yesterday." I paused and fiddled with the hem of my cardigan, trying to compose an answer without throwing my best friend under the bus. "Brittany didn't share the whole truth."

Owen rose and sauntered through the open door of the fishbowl room, poured himself a cup of coffee, and returned to his chair. "Let me guess, Veronica stole manuscripts from more than one author."

I set down the folder with the files and picked up my espresso cup that read **"Guilt cools faster than coffee."**

"I don't know that for sure," I admitted, the words catching in my throat. "It's possible—maybe even likely—but I need more than suspicion. Brittany's research might hold answers… or maybe you can."

Owen ignored my comment and asked, "Do you have all of Veronica's novels here?"

"Of course."

Owen leaned forward, gripping his mug so tight his knuckles went pale. "I think you may be right about her plagiarizing her protégées' manuscripts."

"How do you know?"

"I've listened to every one of her novels, and each one of them is different."

This was not the time to admit I'd only read two of her books. The first one had reminded me of James—I thought it was because he was her mentor at the time. Now I wasn't so sure. The second one just wasn't as good.

Owen stood and wandered back into the fishbowl room, refilling his mug with the last of the pot. I followed, slipping behind the counter to fire up the espresso machine.

"See, every author has a signature—call it a voice, a tone. It's not just *what* you write, it's *how* you do it. The rhythms, the word choices, that intangible 'lens' through which you see the world."

He chugged the rest of his coffee and slammed the mug down. "I learned that from James."

I crossed my arms, brow furrowing. "So you're saying every one of Veronica's twenty novels is different?"

Owen nodded slowly. "Yeah. That's the thing.

They're all technically sharp, sure—but they don't sound the same. Not really. The tone shifts. The rhythm's inconsistent. It's like… they were written by different people."

I felt a chill ripple under my skin, the kind that had nothing to do with fall air. "But her readers never noticed?"

"They were too caught up in the story," he said quietly. "But James noticed. He said it years ago. Told me no one can fake voice forever." Owen's eyes clouded. "Funny thing is—he never said a word about his own novel being stolen. Kept that wound to himself."

He picked up the file folder with "The Sleuths" written on the tab. "Is this Brittany's research?"

"Yes."

The library door swung open, followed by a sugar happy, prancing puppy, and Mary carrying a white pastry box.

"Gabby, how do you keep up with her…" She froze, the leash on her arm extended as far as it would go and Agatha catapulted back to her. "Oh, hi Owen."

"Owen is helping me clear Jame's name."

"In that case," she opened the pastry box. "Have a donut… or two."

Owen thanked her and grabbed a cinnamon cake donut and picked up the file and shook it at me. "Mind if I look at this?"

"Be my guest." With the revelation brewing in my mind, I realized there were more people with a motive to murder Veronica than I originally thought. The real question was, were any of them here at the reading the night Veronica was murdered?

"I'll put the donuts out," Mary offered. "I can tell you're thinking, or whatever you call that blank look."

Agatha hadn't left Mary's side, not only because she hadn't taken the leash off her harness, but because she had a box of donuts.

"No, Agatha, these donuts are for The Sleuths," Mary scolded. Agatha responded by hopping on her hind legs and knocking the box with her nose.

"Sorry, Mary. Let me take those."

"No, Gabby. I can handle her. Go think."

I went to the bookshelves in the mystery section and found the Veronica Steele section. I pulled books two through ten off the shelf. No need to check James's book. On second thought, I grabbed it and joined Owen at a round table where he had the articles spread out.

"What are you doing?" I asked as I placed two stacks on the table.

He held up an article and pointed to a date. "Checking dates of her protégées and her published books."

"You read my mind."

With Dale in jail, surely Detective Brandon would release James this morning. Although I wasn't hunting murder suspects anymore, Owen was convinced he needed to prove James's innocence on the other matter. Just in case Dale was guilty only of remorse—and nothing more. Brandon wasn't going to chase that thread, but I could. We had five minutes before The Sleuths arrived, and we were hot on a list of suspects.

"I'll grab the board." I didn't call it a murder board—these were Veronica's victims, not her killers. Still, among the people who'd gathered for her author reading, it wasn't impossible that one of them belonged on both lists.

"Mind if I cut the names and photos out of these articles?"

"No. I'm sure Brittany can print more copies."

There was no danger of kids coming in today, so I felt safe to set up the board in the middle of the library instead of the fishbowl room. Honestly, I couldn't go in there without keeping the door open since my near-death experience with a cyanide-poisoned candle.

Owen was just hanging the fifth protégée on the board when the main door opened and Bernice, Mabel, and Doris came in clacking like hens.

"Isn't this exciting?"

"We get to sleuth with the Maplewood Miss Marple."

"I hope that handsome James Hatterson is here. He can autograph my book anytime."

"Bernice, he is in prison for murder."

"I can wait. I'll write him letters from the outside."

"You're eighty-five," Mabel reminded her again.

Bernice swung her knitting bag in Mabel's direction. "So?"

Doris sniffed the air. "So? Is that coffee I smell?"

"And donuts?" Bernice added, her knitting needles clacking while she bee-lined for the fishbowl room at a surprising pace for an eighty-five year old.

The hens helped themselves to coffee and donuts. Agatha joined them and they fed the cute little doggy bits of sugar-dusted donut. Within ten minutes, she'd be curled up on her pillow in a sugar coma.

The door chimed again. Good. Finally. The Sleuths were here. No doubt I'd have to make them a fresh pot of coffee and maybe send Mary out for more donuts.

Angela stormed in, phone flashing like a warning beacon, boots clacking with enough purpose to make every powdered donut tremble.

"What have you *done*, Gabrielle Keats?" she shouted, breath fogging up her oversized tortoiseshell glasses. "I just got a call from the *State Library Commission!* I'm going to kill—"

"—whoever forgot the lemon donuts?" Mabel offered innocently, blinking up from her seat like Angela might've just come in for a refill.

Angela narrowed her eyes, clearly not amused. "Don't test me, Mabel."

Bernice set her knitting down with theatrical precision. "Angela, darling, you'll have to get in line. We already promised our next murder-solving effort would be devoted to *Veronica's* killer."

"We're waiting for The Sleuths," Doris added brightly, holding her mug two-handed like it might float away. "They're going to need our expertise."

Angela blinked, thrown for half a beat. "Expertise?"

"Oh, yes," Bernice said, leaning back with a self-satisfied sip. "We've made a list of suspects, motives, and donut preferences. It all ties in, you'll see."

"They think whoever left crumbs in the history aisle might've also left a body," I said, mostly under my breath.

Angela lowered her phone a fraction, lips pressed

tight, like she was weighing whether to play her trump card. Then she aimed the full force of her glare at me.

"Gabrielle, the State Library Commission says someone filed a complaint about me. About the library. Care to explain?"

That got everyone's attention.

Doris gasped so hard I thought she might inhale her donut hole.

"Was it about the time she reclassified the cookbooks under 'dangerous materials'?" Bernice asked.

"That was satirical," Angela snapped.

She pinched the bridge of her nose, but her eyes never left me. "They're sending someone to investigate, Gabby. A field rep. This week."

A stunned hush fell over the room, broken only by Agatha's soft snore from her donut coma.

"Well," Mabel said at last, brushing powdered sugar from her lap. "They better bring donuts."

The hens tittered nervously, but Angela didn't laugh. She leaned across the table, her voice sharp enough to slice through the sugar haze.

"When that rep arrives, Gabrielle, I'll make sure they know exactly who to blame."

CHAPTER 12

FROM SUSPECT LISTS TO STREET FISTS

"PACK UP YOUR BAGS, ladies. We are heading back to Grandview," Angela said to the hens who had settled into comfy leather chairs outside the fishbowl room.

Bernice set the donut she'd been munching on aside and picked up her knitting needles. "We're not going anywhere until James's name is cleared."

Angela huffed and shook her pointer finger at me. "You think you're so… sharp. Like a Miss Marple. Well, let me tell you if I go down, Clarisa goes down with me." She turned back to the hens. "Van leaves in an hour."

The hens ignored her as the main door opened again, letting in a blast of crisp air and a few stray oak leaves.

"Gabby, I came to tell you." Clarisa froze when she saw Angela, standing with hands on both hips, her brown pants suit mirroring the brown oak leaves that had just blown in.

"Why aren't you in jail?" Angela spat.

Clarisa flexed her muscular arms. "I turned myself in but they said I'm free to go."

Remembering how she took Freda down in The Tasty Burger last night, I risked my life and stood between them.

"What did the police say?"

"Your detective fiancé was really sweet."

"Really?"

I thought, when it came to police matters, *sweet* wasn't exactly the word I'd use. *Taciturn*, maybe. *Closed off*. Those fit better.

"Yeah, he helped me call the State Library Commission. I told them everything." When she said the word everything, she leaned around me to see Clarisa's face. "I mean, *everything*."

"Does that mean we get our money back for the tickets?" Bernice asked from behind her, her knitting needles clacking and accenting each word. "I need some extra money for the hotel and food."

I didn't have the heart to tell the hens that even when the Library Commission investigated, it would be a long drawn-out process. If they got their money back, it wouldn't be for years.

"We're staying," Mabel explained. "Until we help The Sleuths solve this murder."

"Yes, that handsome new author is setting up a murder board right now."

Clarisa scanned the board as Owen pinned another photo in place. "Oh—you don't know."

Owen froze, hand still on the pushpin. "Know what?"

Clarisa turned to me, eyebrows raised. "Gabby, you didn't tell them?"

No, I hadn't told them Dale—Veronica's husband—had practically confessed on my front porch yesterday. Then the SWAT team, otherwise known as Greg and Shane, stormed the property and hauled him off in handcuffs.

The door swung open before I could answer, and in sailed Brittany. "Can I publish the article about Dale yet?" Subtlety was never Brittany's strong suit.

It was her turn to freeze, mouth wide open as she took in the room. Me, between Clarisa, her fists still balled, primed for a fight, and Angela, face stern and angry, not backing down. Owen, paused as if he were an old VHS tape. The hens, silent for the first time since I'd met them.

Owen unpaused and looked at me. "What did you not tell us, Gabby?"

Clarisa answered for me. "Dale was arrested last night for Veronica's murder. I only know that because when I went in to talk to Detective Brandon this morning, James was leaving and they were leading Dale to the interrogation room."

"So how do you know he was arrested for murder?" I asked, knowing Detective Brandon wouldn't give information out like that to a virtual stranger. He wouldn't even share that with his fake fiancée.

"Oh, I asked Detective Brandon."

"And he told you?" Brittany challenged.

"Yes, and he was very sweet about my confession. He made me coffee and we sat in a really comfortable room instead of one of those gray interrogation rooms."

Brittany turned on her heel. "I'm going to the police station."

I wanted to go with her. I wanted to look Brandon in the face and ask him why he could be so open with information with strangers but not me. But there was something stopping me. Someone. James. He was free.

Out of nowhere, he walked through the door just as Brittany swept out. He looked more like himself—clean-shaven, crisp white shirt, his signature cologne trailing behind him.

I abandoned my post as referee between Angela and Clarisa and gave him a bear hug. Before I released him, he murmured, "Gabby, I need to talk to you."

"Sure, but first you need to see what Owen is doing." I hooked his elbow and steered him toward the board.

"Veronica did steal your manuscript, and you are not the only victim."

The hens shot up, clucking with relief, crowding James like he'd come home to roost.

"Good," he said. "We're going to need these."

"Need what?" Mabel asked.

James tipped his fedora. "Ladies." The hens backed up a step, giving him room, before he turned to me. "More suspects."

"I told you we should stay in town," Bernice added, smiling up at James, her cornflower-blue eyes twinkling until they all but disappeared in the folds of her wrinkles.

Doris added, "And you also said there was another body in the history section."

"There are. Millions. All those wars and despots."

"You said literally."

"I said literaturely," Bernice responded.

"That's not a word," Mabel said.

"I know—I was just trying to keep the hype going." Bernice raised both hands in the air and gave them a little pump, like a cheerleader whose pom-poms had been replaced by knitting needles.

"You don't even know what that means," Mabel shot back.

I turned my attention from the hens and swiveled to face James. "You said you needed to talk to me?"

James took my elbow this time and motioned to Owen to join us. "Let's go back to your office."

The hens continued to argue. I interrupted. "Help yourself to more donuts and coffee."

The front door swished open again.

"This library is like Grand Central station," Mabel offered. "So much more friendly than Grandview."

It was then that I realized I'd left Clarisa and Angela to duke it out. Angela didn't stand a chance with her bony wiry body, devoid of any muscle.

Thomas slipped off his wool coat and draped it neatly over the back of a chair. "That other librarian, Angela? She looked pretty upset."

Antonio, already tugging at his scarf and puffing from the cold, slapped his hands together like punctuation. "Her assistant was chasing her down the street."

Oh great. Clarisa hadn't gone to jail, *yet*.

"I'll be right back."

"Where are you going?" James called from across the library.

"To prevent another murder—or at least a savage beating."

I grabbed my coat from the hook and asked Mary to keep an eye on Agatha, still in a sugar coma in her bed in the corner.

It wasn't hard to spot Angela and Clarisa—the only two women barreling down the middle of Main Street, shrieking at each other like banshees. By the time I caught up at the town square, Clarisa had already body-slammed Angela flat on the brick walkway.

"You won't get away with this," Angela yelled.

I tapped Clarisa lightly on the back in case she had one of those knee-jerk reactions. She did have one of those knee-jerk reactions and elbowed me in the nose. As blood spurted out, she turned and a switch flipped to the off position.

"Oh Gabby! I..."

Angela slithered her wiry figure out from under Clarisa and stood and dusted herself off. Dead leaves and a few twigs rained down on the grass. "You're going to jail."

"You're going to jail," Clarisa shot back and steeled herself for another attack.

Meanwhile, the blood continued to spurt from my nose. The front of my burgundy coat now bore a spreading brown stain, its round edges ballooning outward until it looked like a lopsided pumpkin. Trust me to wear autumn colors and end up decorated for the season.

"Ladies." They both turned to me. "I think I'm..." I fell to the ground. Sure, I was faking it, but passing out was the only thing I could think of doing right now.

As I lay on the ground with my eyes closed there was a shuffling of leaves. Clarisa knelt beside me and commanded, "Call 911."

Tires shrieked, the bite of burnt rubber filling the air. I cracked one eye open as Brittany's red Toyota 4Runner skidded to a stop, engine growling.

"What did you do to her?" She leapt out and helped me to my feet, then handed me the bandana she had wrapped around her hair.

"You." She pointed to Clarisa. "In the back seat."

"You too," she pointed to Angela.

She settled me in the front seat and pushed the bandana into my nostrils. "Keep your head back."

I put my hand over the bandana and closed my eyes again.

Brittany slammed my door, muttering under her breath. "I don't know why I had to get a job in Grandview. This town has enough stories to publish a violent act or murder once a day."

She opened her door and slid into the driver's seat, hitting the start button with much more aggression than necessary.

As she backed into traffic, she said, "Gabby, would you stop confronting murderers?

"We didn't murder anyone," Clarisa said from the backseat.

Brittany glanced in the rearview mirror. "You just tried to murder my best friend."

"No… I just elbowed her in the nose."

"Hard enough to break it?"

I pulled the shade down and glanced in the mirror.

Where my nose should have been was a swollen, misshapen mass of flesh.

"My nose is broken?" I said, which sounded more like "mmm no bwok en."

Brittany glanced in the rearview mirror again. "What do you have to say for yourself, Miss Fancy Pants Suit?"

Angela responded by crossing her arms and scowling.

"Okay, have it your way. They have ways of making you talk." She sped into the police station parking lot and slammed on the brake, skidding to a stop. She smashed the car into park.

"Let's go girls."

"You're turning us in?" Angela asked incredulously. "It was just a little misunderstanding."

"Oh I forgot. You are under arrest. I'm sure they'll read you your rights inside."

She pulled out her camera and snapped a photo of my purple face and then one of each of Angela and Clarisa.

"Oh, and enjoy the piece I'm writing for The Grandview Gazette this afternoon. I'm still trying to think of a good headline. *Librarians Attack Librarian In The Town Square?* Or *Attempted Murder of Local Favorite Librarian Thwarted By The Press.* By "by the press" I mean me."

I waited in the car while Brittany marched Clarisa and Angela into the police station. My nose had stopped bleeding, but it was definitely broken. I pulled my phone out and texted James.

Start The Sleuths Meeting Without Me.
I have been delayed.

There was no way I was telling him I'd been delayed by another crime. A violent crime conducted by Clarisa's knee-jerk reaction—make that elbow. It made me wonder how she had submitted to Angela all this time. Maybe her pent up anger was finally releasing in socially unacceptable ways.

James texted back.

> We need you. The hens are pecking at me.

I giggled. Then groaned from the pain.I could imagine them surrounding him and pelting him with not only compliments, but Bernice was most likely suggesting totally inappropriate things.

Someone rapped on the window. I rolled it down.

"Hwello, Bwandon," I said.

"She beat the crap out of you." He opened the door, I think to give me a hug but Brittany joined us and pulled him back.

"Take a step back. This is my best friend and I'm taking her to the hospital."

"And this is my fault?"

"Yes, you let that testosterone-loaded angry muscle-bound woman out of jail."

"An wou tole er bout Dale,"

"You won't share information with your fiancée or the press, but line up violent offenders and you share all."

"What? I.." He backed up with both hands in the air, as if he were surrendering.

"I'm taking her to the hospital." She jogged around

to the driver's side and opened the door. "I'm publishing the article about Dale and then later, a great one on the incompetence of the police."

She didn't give him time to answer, but sped out of the parking lot to the hospital.

CHAPTER 13
A NOSE FOR TROUBLE

I STRAINED at the seatbelt and jiggled the door handle. "Wait, take me back to the library. James said he had something he needed to tell me in private."

I sounded as if I had a mouthful of peanut butter. I'm sure the only reason Brittany understood what I was saying is because she was my best friend and had spent countless hours with me.

Brittany clicked the lock button on her side. "Are you crazy? It looks like someone took a meat tenderizer to your face. We are going to the hospital."

I tried to give her my puppy dog eyes, but it wasn't working.

Puppy dog eyes. Agatha!

I pulled out my phone and called the front desk at the library. "Hey, Mary. I'b on my way to the hospidal," I said, my swollen lip turning *hospital* into something out of a toddler's first word list.

"What?"

"Yeah, I …"

"Give me that phone." Brittany reached over and grabbed the phone. "Mary. Brittany here. Clarisa broke Gabby's nose. I'm taking her to the hospital. Can you take care of Agatha?" She paused for a response.

"Thangk you. Can you ged James on da phone?" I mumbled.

She didn't even blink, clearly used to translating me when I sounded like I'd gone bobbing for apples and forgot to let go.

She glanced at me and pointed to my face. I took that gesture to mean "you might want to check your face." I pulled down the visor and stared at a swollen, purple version of my face. My eyes were pinched into slits, and the whole effect gave serious "blueberry muffin meets bad decisions" energy.

On second thought, stopping at the library to talk to James was off the table. *Did I look like this when Brandon saw me?* A giant pummeled blueberry muffin face?

"Did I look like this when you intercepted Brandon's hug?"

"You're worried about that? He didn't tell you about Dale." Then she thought better of it and added, "No, you looked a little less like that. More like a large purple grape with slits."

"Thanks." I shut the visor and leaned back in my seat and closed my eyes, which wasn't difficult since they were barely slits anyway. On to the hospital, where I hoped they could give me something for the swelling.

"That's it, just relax. The Sleuths are going to meet us at the hospital. James can talk to us then."

She pulled into the portico nearest the emergency room and threw the Toyota 4Runner in park. "Let's go,

Miss Marple. May I point out she never gets in-between two psychos?"

"No, she just sits in the room with them and knits while they incriminate themselves."

She reached over and unbuckled me as if I were a child. "That was your plan at The Tasty Burger, right? And who was the only one who incriminated themself?"

"Clairisa?"

"Why are you asking that as if it were a question? You know it is true. And yet, you followed her to the town square."

"She was going to kill Angela."

"And she would have been arrested, gone to jail, and you would still have a face."

"I see your point." But I couldn't let it go. "But you go after the truth. You ask the hard questions. You print articles that could get you killed."

I opened my door and stepped out gingerly, so as not to jar my head too much.

"The key word is print. I type up articles and send them out on the internet. I don't *actually* chase down murderers."

"I don't chase them. They show up at my house or the library."

Brittany joined me and clicked the lock button on her Toyota 4Runner.

She took me by the elbow and led me to the sliding glass doors.

"Oh my, Brittany, who do we have here?"

"Stop it, Bella. You know who this is."

She leaned closer and studied my smashed blueberry muffin face. "Gabby, is that you? Did Brandon do that to you? I really dodged a bullet on that one."

She shoved me into a wheelchair, jarring my head and making it feel like a spiced pumpkin scone that was over-baked, dropped, and then served anyway on the good china. As Miss Marple would say, *"Some people hide malice behind manners. Others just prefer to serve it with whipped cream and a fake smile."*

Brittany leaned closer to Bella's ear, her voice low but deliberately loud enough for the ER lobby to catch every word.

"No, Brandon didn't do this to her, so don't you even whisper that rumor. And just so we're clear—I could print how you were involved in that medication-override scandal last year. Nearly lost your license after a patient nearly arrested over an overdose. Want to see *that* headline?"

Bella paled and wheeled me to the front desk. "Jenna, this is Gabby Keats."

Jenna stood and leaned over the counter. "No it is not."

She gasped and raised a hand to her mouth. "Yes, it is her. I would recognize her vintage vibe anywhere."

"I can talk," I offered, rising from the chair with more confidence than sense. "Broken nose. Not broken—"

The words fizzled as the room tilted. Not dramatically, not in a cinematic swoon—more like the slow, lazy swirl of cartoon flies orbiting my head.

Then everything lurched.

I sat down hard, and my nose—apparently feeling left out of the drama—chose that exact moment to erupt like Old Faithful. Warmth spilled over my lip, hot and coppery, and I slapped a hand over it, already regretting my attempt at standing like a normal adult.

"That's enough talk," Brittany instructed. "Get her back to where a professional can work on her."

Bella opened her mouth to object, but Brittany—channeling the Ghost of Christmas Present—silenced her with one long, pointed finger. Meanwhile, I was too busy gagging on the warm, metallic rush of blood sliding down my throat to appreciate the theatrics.

A stern-faced doctor in pressed scrubs appeared in the sliding glass doors. He looked to be in his mid-fifties, salt-and-pepper hair, arms folded like he'd yet to be impressed by this ER's theatrics.

"This patient needs cautery," he said curtly as Brittany guided me in. He nodded to Bella and the other nurse—then, with an air of "I'll handle it," led me to a stainless-steel exam table beneath a glaring overhead lamp.

He had me tip my head back slightly—just enough so the bright light caught the droplets still forming by my nostrils. The scent of antiseptic mix with warm copper filled the air.

"Topical anesthetic and vasoconstrictor," he murmured as he unwrapped a cotton-soaked pledget, pressing it gently in my nostril for half a minute. I tasted the faint bitterness of lidocaine—numbing relief edged with panic.

He pulled something thin and white from his kit. "This will sting," he warned, still not meeting my eyes. A sharp burn flared as he pressed it to my nose, followed by the faintest hiss—like a match snuffed out too soon. My eyes watered, my heart jumped, and then…silence. The bleeding had stopped.

He loosened his gloves. "I'll give you something for pain and swelling."

With practiced efficiency, he injected what he called a mild opioid and a corticosteroid. I felt warmth in my arm as the meds slid in.

He cleared his throat. "Swelling's going to have to subside—there's nothing more we can do for your face right now. Just rest, ice, and let the meds work." His tone was clipped, almost clinical, but not unkind.

Bella hovered nearby. He glanced at her. "Follow post-care instructions: nasal ointment, no NSAIDs, no blowing your nose. If it bleeds again, pinch for fifteen minutes and come back." He paused like he expected her to record every word. "Understand?"

Bella nodded.

He looked at me, lifting an eyebrow. "You'll feel soreness for a few days. Otherwise, you're good to go." He gave one small nod and moved on, like he was late for rounds.

I sat up and slid off the table.

Brittany pulled back the curtain. "The Sleuths are here."

She gave one more warning glance to Bella and pretended to type midair.

Bella nodded and slipped out through the curtain, the rings whispering along the track. It was quiet out there—the kind of quiet that said my mashed-up face was the most excitement this ER had seen all day.

I took the prescription the other nurse handed me and shuffled out to the waiting room where The Sleuths and the hens waited. Apparently, James couldn't shake them, or knowing him, he was too nice *not* to invite them along.

"Oh my dear," James said, shaking his head as Brittany rushed me through the automatic doors. "I won't hug you. Take a seat."

He guided me toward a row of turquoise pleather chairs bolted to the floor, each one squeaking just enough to make a point. I eased down, trying not to jar anything that might still be attached to my face.

"Clarisa did this," Brittany announced, folding her arms. "I want to squash any rumors before they get started."

I shifted, wincing.

"She didn't do it on purpose," I said quietly. "It was... sort of an accident."

Antonio frowned, squinting at me like my face was a puzzle piece from the wrong box. "How do you do *that* by accident?" He tilted his head. "It looks like someone tried to hand-toss your face like pizza dough...but forgot to catch it."

"You are so right, Antonio," Bernice offered. "That face says someone pummeled you on purpose."

"Are you glad we landed in the middle of a mystery now?" Mabel chided.

"Not if it means our favorite librarian gets her face replaced with a rotten plum," Bernice returned, whipping out her knitting needles. "What happened to the other librarians? The swindler and miniature Amazon woman?"

"You mean Angela and Clarisa?" Doris corrected.

"They are in jail."

Bernice clacked her needles together. "Bout time."

Emory, Randolph, and Thomas had been silent up to this point. Not that they could get a word in edgewise.

The emergency room doors swished open again and Emily, Veronica's protege slipped in.

She spotted Brittany and said, "Oh I think I came in the wrong door."

Thomas stood and addressed her."Which door were you looking for?"

"Oh I got some lab work done the other day. I came to get the results."

"Dr. Emory can show you the way," Thomas suggested and motioned to Emory, who turned a lovely shade of red, like the red maples outside the entrance.

Dr. Emory stood and fumbled with his hands as if he didn't know what to do with them. He finally shoved them in his pockets. "I … umm. Sure."

Good. Emory. Get a new crush. Not only is your other crush—me—taken, I think, but I currently look like an exploded grape and smell like one of the cadavers in your lab. Not exactly romantic hero material.

Emory took off down the hallway, his long, awkward limbs flailing slightly as he hustled toward the elevators. He pressed the up button with more determination than grace. Emily jogged to catch up, her steps quick but no match for Emory's enthusiastic stride. It was like watching a stork outpace a gazelle.

I knew because I was watching. So was everyone else in the waiting room, heads swiveling like we were tuned in to a live K-drama rerun. All Emily needed to do was trip in slow motion and land perfectly in

Emory's outstretched arms. With his gangly build and nervous energy, he'd probably catch her, apologize for touching her, and then write a report about it.

After they got on the elevator, no fall included, I turned to James. "What did you want to tell me?"

He looked around the waiting room. "You want me to tell you here?"

"If you don't tell her right now, you'll have to wait until tomorrow," Randolph said, finally stepping into the conversation with the finality of a man used to being in scrubs and obeyed. "She needs to rest. That's my professional medical opinion."

Bernice, Mabel, and Doris shook their heads in synchronized dismay, as if they'd rehearsed it on the drive over. Bernice's knitting needles clicked softly in her lap, already halfway through what looked like a very opinionated tea cozy.

"We could come sit with her," Bernice offered, peering over her glasses.

My head hurt too much to shake in protest. The last thing I needed was a rotating trio of well-meaning commentary and passive-aggressive blanket tucking.

"I'll take care of her," Brittany intervened, saving me from a cackling afternoon guaranteed to rob me of rest.

James paced a few steps, then turned toward me. "I spent the night in the same cell as Dale. He didn't murder his wife."

I blinked at him. "Then why did he say 'If only you would have told me... I wouldn't have...?'"

"He meant he wouldn't have had her declared incompetent," James said. "Or whatever the legal term is. He thought he was protecting her."

Brittany's expression shifted. "Protecting her from what?"

James hesitated, the tension pulling tight like a dropped stitch in Bernice's knitting.

"She was hiding something," he said finally. "Something big."

CHAPTER 14
A FLOCK OF SLEUTHS

BRITTANY LED me to her Toyota 4Runner in the parking lot as if I was one of the toddlers attending story hour. Once I was seated, she leaned over and buckled my seatbelt.

Buckling me in was a little bit overkill, but I didn't mind. It gave me more time to think. What if the thing Veronica was hiding was the very thing Owen and I were investigating? Maybe his theory was right and she'd never written a book, and faced with her own mortality, she was ready to come clean.

Hadn't Dale told me there were odd payments going out of their bank account? Maybe her guilt got the best of her and she was trying to make retribution starting with leaving half of her estate to James, the one whose book launched her writing career.

Brittany moved to her side of the Toyota 4Runner and as she had her hand on the handle, Brandon came up to my window out of the blue and tapped on it.

"Hey, wait."

"We're not talking to you," Brittany yelled across the top of the vehicle.

"What is this? Kindergarten?"

"You started it, but sharing pertinent information with other girls on the playground," Brittany shot back.

I rolled down the window.

"Oh my gosh, Gabby. Your face."

I rolled the window back up.

"Yep. I'll say it again—the testosterone-laden embezzler you released this morning did that."

She slammed her door, pushed the start button, shoved it into gear and left Brandon standing in the parking lot. I turned to watch him as The Sleuths, the hens, and Emily exited the building.

Emily was smiling. Was she smiling because she liked Emory? That would be good. Nope. She wasn't looking at him but at a piece of paper she grasped with both hands.

"Brittany, have you interviewed Emily yet?" I asked, twisting to face her in the passenger seat.

She threw me a sideways glance. "That's what you want to talk about?"

I shrugged. "Just wondering."

Brittany tapped her fingers on the steering wheel. "How about we talk about the case and Detective Brandon?"

I crossed my arms. "This might be important to the case."

She gripped the steering wheel with both hands, her knuckles whitening. "How about we toilet paper the trees in front of his house?"

"What?" I blinked and adjusted my seatbelt, trying

to decide if she was serious. As irritated as I was at Brandon, Brittany was acting like we were in kinder-garten—or maybe middle school.

"No, really," I said, leaning back. "Something about her…"

"She was Veronica's protégé," Brittany interrupted, her tone flat. "Veronica's death upset her and she couldn't do the interview. End of story."

I frowned, looking out the window as the quiet street passed by. "But why would she have medical testing done in a small town when she could go back to Grandview with a larger hospital?"

"I don't know." Brittany's voice softened just a touch.

I didn't either, but I was going to find out.

"Where is my phone?"

"It's in the glove compartment." She nodded toward it without taking her eyes off the road.

I popped open the compartment and pulled it out, my fingers moving quickly to send a text to Emory.

What did Emily have tests run for?

His reply was quick.

I have no idea.

I stared at the screen. He was officially fired from The Sleuths.

Brittany pulled up in front of my house and threw the car into park. "Go on in. I asked Miranda to check on you later. I'll pick up Agatha and keep her for the rest of the day."

I paused, my hand on the door handle. What happened to *I'll take care of her*? Or was this her way of saving me from the hens? Maybe I didn't need saving. In the middle of their clucking and casserole offers, there could be actual clues. In fact, I had a great idea.

I turned toward her. "What are you going to do?"

She shifted in her seat and pulled her scarf tighter. "I have a few stories to work on. One about Dale to amend. Another about the Grandview librarians."

I unbuckled and opened the door partway, the cold air rushing in. Then I paused. "I changed my mind. I do want the hens to come over."

"You do?" Brittany tilted her head, her blue eyes scanning my face. "What are you up to, Miss Marple?"

"I'm thinking of taking up knitting. Bernice is really good at it."

Brittany scoffed. "Did you see that tea cozy she was knitting? No one uses them anymore."

I grinned, one foot already on the curb.

"You were joking," she said, narrowing her eyes.

"Was I?" I winked and shut the door.

Once inside, I clicked on The Tasty Burger app and put in an order for four. Then I called Bernice at the Airbnb.

"Still up for babysitting a girl with a battered face?"

Instead of answering me, she held the phone away from her mouth and yelled. "Doris, Mabel, Gabby needs us."

Then muffled conversation.

"James, could you take us to Gabby's?"

Someone slammed the receiver down ending the call.

I continued to stare at the phone for a moment before I laughed. Then stopped because my face hurt. I thought I was going to enjoy hanging out with the hens.

Ten minutes later, James tapped on the door with a, "Gabby, I'm here with your… he… guests."

"Come in." I'd taken the time to change and throw my wool coat into a garbage bag. I'd have to go back to Second Hand Chic and find a replacement. If I tried to wash the blood out, the coat would probably disintegrate from age alone.

James pushed the door open and Bernice led the charge, squeezing under his arm, her knitting bag slung around her neck. Doris and Mabel followed, a little less nimble on their feet. Mabel held a pastry box.

"We don't have any chicken noodle soup, but we do have donuts!" She held the box up like a trophy.

James ran a hand over his face. He must be exhausted from his ordeal. I couldn't let him leave just yet. I needed to ask him one question.

"Thank you, ladies, there are platters in the kitchen." I pointed in that direction as the parade of knitwear and strong opinions bustled through.

Bernice set her knitting bag on the coffee table. "We'll take care of everything."

I sank into the sofa and patted the seat next to me. "I just have one question, and then you can go home, James."

From the kitchen, bits of conversation drifted out like a radio set to Local Gossip FM.

"Look at these dishes—you'd think she was our age."

"You mean *your* age," Mabel said, clearly offended.

"I know I'm eighty-five. You don't have to remind me every five minutes."

"Look, ladies, we need to clean this coat for her."

James blinked. "Did she say—your coat?"

I sighed happily. "Mm-hmm."

"In the trash?"

I nodded. "It was a tragic loss. A blood stain the size of Agatha." I pointed to my nose, the obvious source.

"They're cleaning a coat you threw away?"

"Of course. You don't think they'd let a perfectly good wool blend meet its end without intervention, do you?"

He glanced toward the kitchen, wide-eyed, as a drawer opened and a cheer went up.

"Here's the coffee maker!"

"I'll make the coffee."

James turned back to me slowly, like a man realizing he was no longer in control of his life. "I feel... thoroughly hen-pecked."

I smiled. "Welcome to the club. You should feel honored. They don't hen-peck just anyone."

I gave James a moment, letting the sounds of drawer-rummaging and enthusiastic hen-chatter fill the silence. Then I asked quietly, "So... why did Detective Brandon release you?"

James sighed. "He said he was following a new lead. I was free to go, but not to leave town."

My brow knit. "What was the lead?"

He hesitated, then said flatly, "Dale."

I blinked. "Dale? As in…currently in jail for almost confessing to murder on my lawn, Dale?"

James raised both brows in solidarity. "The very same. Which makes zero sense. Unless Brandon's just walking in narrative circles for sport."

I crossed my arms. "That man doesn't just muddy the waters—he stirs them with a canoe paddle."

James gave a quiet chuckle, but his eyes stayed serious.

"Well," I said, leaning forward, "while he's throwing darts in the dark, Owen and I were building something useful. A timeline. We've been matching the dates Veronica's books were published with when each of her protégées was under her wing."

James straightened a bit. "You think someone else had a manuscript stolen?"

"I'm sure of it. Veronica's mentorship pattern is too regular, and the similarities in those debut novels? Not coincidence. If we can prove she borrowed from more than one protégé a little too liberally…"

"It could shift the whole motive landscape."

"Exactly." I tapped my fingers on the armrest. "Brandon's looking at this like a single betrayal. But what if it was a cycle? A trail of resentment?"

James exhaled. "He'll never see it coming."

From the kitchen, someone called, "Where does she keep her cinnamon sticks?"

"In the drawer marked *herbs and sassy intentions*," I called back, which earned a flutter of laughter.

James shook his head. "I'm in a house full of knitting detectives, and somehow you're the least terrifying one."

I grinned. "Don't count on it."

Mabel entered the living room with a tray of mugs and a coffee carafe. "Here you go."

"I think this is my time to exit," James said, rising with a groan and stretching before reaching for his coat. He tipped his hat as he slid it back onto his head, the brim slightly crooked. "But keep an eye on this one," he added, nodding toward me with mock solemnity.

I raised an eyebrow. "I'm right here, you know."

"She has you here for more than caretaking, coffee, and conversation," he said, pulling on one sleeve, then the other. "Don't let the cozy veneer fool you."

He gave his hat a final, firm push into place and headed for the door.

"Escape while you can," I called after him, smiling.

He saluted without turning around.

The door clicked shut behind him, and almost instantly, Bernice swept in from the kitchen carrying a polished tray stacked with donuts and pride. "So," she said, eyes twinkling, "do you have some sleuthing for us to do?"

I pushed a stack of coasters aside and leaned forward. "I do. But let's save those donuts for after lunch, or we'll be in a sugar fog all afternoon. I'll explain the plan in full detail soon—but first, we need to get Agatha back."

"Ooooh, a séance!" Doris called from somewhere behind the fridge. "Agatha Christie, we summon thee!"

"That's the *dog's* name, Doris," Bernice said without even turning, already pouring coffee like a professional diner waitress. "And she responds better to donuts than candlelight."

I took the mug she handed me and grinned. "True. But I'm not ruling out mystical intervention. With the way this case is going, I might need a little ghostly insight."

"Well," Mabel said, appearing with a lemon-scented dish towel draped over one arm like a maître d', "we've got time, caffeine, and absolutely no regard for minding our own business. You've come to the right flock."

CHAPTER 15
UNDERCOVER WITH THE HENS

WE'D FINISHED OUR LUNCH, picked up Agatha, and now the hens and I were squeezed into my buttercream-yellow VW Bug. I had thrown on a pair of sunglasses and a floppy hat. No doubt everyone in town recognized my car, and me for that matter. So I planned to park behind City Hall in the gravel lot while I sent the hens on their assignments.

I dropped Bernice and Mabel off at The Daily Grind, while Mabel walked Agatha around the town square. All three promised to report to me within the hour.

I settled into my seat with an Agatha Christie book: *The Murder at the Vicarage*—the perfect small-town whodunit set in St. Mary Mead, featuring Miss Marple's genteel detective skills amidst a cozy-yet-quiet village.

The passenger door opened, startling me enough to reach into the center console for mace. I pulled out hand sanitizer. Fine. I could squirt it in the intruder's eyes.

"I saw two of your Miss Marples at The Daily Grind."

I pulled my hat down further, trying to hide my face. "Brandon."

"Why are you hiding from me?"

My indignation overcame my embarrassment. I whipped my hat and glasses off. "Really?" I leaned closer to him. "This. Not to mention the fact you shared information about Dale's arrest with the woman who did this."

"I'm sorry."

"And since when are you 'nice' and 'sweet' at the police station," I pressed, trying to think of Clarisa's exact words.

"When I think using those tactics will get a suspect to open up and share information."

I leaned back, pressing my throbbing head against the headrest. "Oh." *What sort of information could an embezzling assistant librarian give about a murder case?* I wanted to ask the question. But I was too angry. And maybe channeling some of my Brittany-vibes. "You should try that tactic with your girlfriend."

"You have information you're withholding about the murder case?"

"No. I did what you told me. I focused on the librarians—and you see how that turned out." It was like I'd wandered into a harvest festival expecting cider and cinnamon donuts, and instead got caught in a runaway hayride driven by sugar-crazed squirrels. Right over my face.

He put a hand on the door. "Okay, well, see you later then."

See you later? What?

What happened to the "be nice to your girlfriend"

advice? Or was it only important to be nice if I had information regarding the case? He didn't even bring me a coffee.

Of course, I didn't give him the list of potential suspects Owen had sent me photos of. We weren't one hundred percent sure they were suspects. As Brandon crunched across the gravel parking lot, Owen called me on FACETIME.

I pushed the answer button.

He gasped. "Oh… Gabby,"

"It's just a broken nose. What did you learn?"

He stopped looking at me and turned the camera on the suspect board. "Every single publication date coincides with a mentorship ending shortly before."

"So you think she stole manuscripts from every single person she mentored?"

"It looks that way. But I don't want to jump to conclusions."

"Yep. I get that. That's how James ended up in jail."

"Have you talked to Detective Brandon recently?"

I shifted in my seat. "Define 'talked.'"

He sat down and leaned the phone up against something, probably a cup of coffee. "Do you know what's going on with the case?"

"No. I just talked to him and he's not telling me anything."

"Did you two have a fight?"

"Not really. We're just not communicating well right now."

"Want my advice?" he asked, rubbing his hand over his chin.

"Sure."

"Keep your private life separate from your relationship."

Wise words coming from such a young man. Maybe he was right, though. It wasn't my job to tell Brandon how to treat suspects. He didn't tell me how to run book club or story hour.

"That's great advice, Owen."

The passenger door opened again. "Thought you could use a coffee," Brandon said. "Oh hey, Owen."

"I thought you left."

"I did because I noticed you were reading and you didn't have a coffee. I imagine you probably plan to be here for a while."

"Thank you. That was sweet of you."

"Did you tell him?" Owen asked, reminding me he was still here. He didn't need to worry about me kissing Brandon, not in this condition.

"No. Why don't you fill him in."

Owen filled Detective Brandon in on the entire plagiarism theory and I followed up with what Dale had told me about the odd payments going out.

"So you think she was trying to make amends to the writers she allegedly stole manuscripts from?"

"Yes."

"Well, we'd have to prove she actually stole them. And see if any of them took her to court."

"James and I are heading to Grandview tomorrow to search the public records for court cases. Copyright infringement, maybe a motion to dismiss, if it got that far."

"I'll contact some of the latest protégés and see if they'll talk to me." Just then, Emily slipped out the back door of the courthouse, pausing just long enough to scan the lot like she suspected someone might be listening. Her boots crunched over the gravel as she hurried toward her car. "I know just where to start."

I placed my hat back on my head, though the sunglasses stayed in the car—they pinched my face like rubber bands. "Mind waiting here for a few minutes?" I asked, cracking my car door open.

"I'll be here talking to Owen."

"Emily, wait up!" I called as she headed for her car.

She turned, startled, then kept walking. I jogged, ignoring the throb in my face, and reached her just as her key fob chirped.

"Just one question."

She looked ready to bolt, so I dove right in.

"Did Veronica Steele steal a manuscript from you?"

Her eyes welled instantly. She fished out a tissue and dabbed at her lashes. "How did you—? So it's true what they say about you."

"What do they say?"

"That you're some sort of Agatha Christie supersleuth," she said, smoothing a dark wave of hair over her shoulder. "I was just inside, trying to file something —maybe a civil complaint. I don't know. I figured I'd need a lawyer to help draft the actual claim. Something about breach of intellectual property. Or maybe even petitioning for a temporary injunction."

"Why didn't you want Brittany to interview you?" I asked changing the subject.

"Because, who would believe me now? If Veronica were alive, I could get a temporary injunction and stop publication. People might believe me. But she's dead and all her fans, including that crazy Freda-podcast-chick will think I made it up."

"You're not the only one, you know."

"So it is true about James Hatterson, then? He paid her off, but she stole his work?"

"Yes, and allegedly many more."

She glanced toward my VW Bug and froze. "Wait— is that the detective sitting in your car?"

I followed her gaze. Sure enough, Brandon was still in the front seat of Buttercup, watching the parking lot like a bored hawk. His FACETIME call with Owen must have ended.

"Can we just hang back a minute?" she asked, her voice dropping. "I really don't want to walk past him. My nerves are shot."

She looked more skittish than a stray cat Agatha had chased behind the library once or twice—or maybe three times.

"Just one last piece of advice?" I offered gently. "I'd suggest you do that interview with Brittany, because I have it on good authority she'll have more writers who are in the same situation as you."

"Whose authority?"

"Mine."

She chuckled. "I feel better already. I'll call her."

She got in her car and with a quick wave pulled out of the parking lot.

I walked slowly back to mine, trying not to jar my face. The pain meds I'd taken earlier had worn off and so had the adrenaline that had carried through the afternoon and my crazy hens sleuthing plan.

"You look beat," Brandon said as I slid in the driver's seat. "Sorry. Poor choice of words."

I laughed out of delirium, exhaustion, or both.

"How about I take you home?"

"What about the hens and Agatha?"

"I'll stop at the Daily Grind and the town square after I get you home. I can fill the ladies in."

"And Agatha?"

"I'll bring her over when I bring dinner."

"Oh."

"Now climb in the back…"

I stifled a laugh. "I really don't feel like making out." Not that I'd ever made out in the back of Buttercup—or any car, for that matter. My love life had the energy of a bookmarked bad mystery novel: occasionally revisited, rarely finished.

I maneuvered in with all the grace of a library cart hitting a loose rug. I meant to slide in smoothly. Instead, I ended up flopped on my side, both feet still sticking out the door like a broken marionette.

Brandon raised an eyebrow. "Whatever the doctor gave you is making you loopy."

"I'm fine," I said, still half-laughing. "This is just how I get in cars now. It's a system."

He didn't respond, but I caught the smirk he tried—and failed—to hide as he gently pushed my feet inside and shut the door behind me.

Brandon started the car and then made a phone call. "Yeah, Shane, I need you to pick me up at Gabby's in ten minutes."

I couldn't hear the response but Brandon's retort made it clear it wasn't appropriate.

"No I did not…we did not… Just come pick me up." He pressed the end button. Seconds later, it seemed, we pulled up to my house and he helped me inside.

———

I slept so hard, the slobber dried on my chin—a tragically undignified badge of painkiller-induced oblivion. My limbs felt like they'd been poured in concrete, and when I shifted on the couch, a bolt of fire shot through my nose, reminding me—loudly—that it was still broken.

The sun was setting, painting the living room walls in soft gold, though even that seemed too bright for my pounding head. My tongue felt like it had grown a wool sweater, and I was ninety percent sure I'd drooled through it.

The doorbell chimed.

I jolted, then immediately regretted it. My equilibrium wobbled and I stumbled to my feet, catching myself on the coffee table just before I went nose-first into the carpet. Which, in hindsight, would've been adding insult to literal injury.

"That would've been painful," I muttered, pressing a hand gently to the bridge of my nose. Still tender. Still not ready for guests.

"We're here with dinner!" Bernice's voice floated in through the door, chipper and commanding. Of course they came.

The door swung open and Brandon led the procession with brown paper bags with The Tasty Burger logo sticker on them.

"We couldn't leave you alone," Bernice announced. "Right, ladies?" She settled in a chair and pulled out her knitting.

"Hmm," Doris murmured, her tone thoughtful. She pulled a tissue out of her purse and gently examined my nose.

"Looks like your septum might be deviated—either from the break or something you were born with that got knocked further out of place."

She paused.

"That can cause one-sided congestion, headaches, maybe even snoring or restless sleep," she added.

"You're a nurse?" I asked as she studied my face.

"She *was* a nurse. For forty years at Grandview Memorial Hospital," Bernice interjected, her knitting needles clacking.

Doris ignored her and kept going. "First—keep your nasal passages calm. Saline rinse once or twice a day. If you're still stuffy, try a nasal steroid like Flonase for a week or two."

She gave me a kind smile. "Maybe a decongestant, but just for a few days. And a humidifier by your bed wouldn't hurt, especially with all that mouth-breathing."

I nodded slowly, still foggy.

"But," she added, voice firm now, "if you're getting sinus headaches or still not sleeping right—see an ENT. Septoplasty can straighten things out. It's outpatient and pretty routine."

She rested a weathered hand on my shoulder. "For now, take it slow. Saline. Steroid spray. Humidifier. Ice if it gets swollen. And let us know as soon as you need more help. You're not alone."

Nope. I'd never be alone with Brandon. Ever. Not that I wanted a romantic dinner with an overripe plum for a nose. I would like to finish our conversation from earlier in the parking lot and apologize for my overreaction to his being nice to Clarisa. It wasn't his fault she was a loose canon. Why did he want her to hear about Dale?

Doris and Mabel busied themselves in the kitchen putting the food on "real plates."

"Look at this vintage plate," Mabel said, her tone reverent. "Scalloped edge, hand-painted violets—oh, this is Coalport if I've ever seen it. You could serve lemon shortbread on this and feel like royalty."

Doris let out a small hmmph. "It's lovely, but there's a hairline crack near the rim. I wouldn't trust it with anything runnier than mashed potatoes."

Brandon raised an eyebrow at me. "Do I want to know how many plates you own?"

I shrugged. "They come from estate sales and secondhand shops. Each one's got a story. And apparently, an appraisal committee."

Bernice, curled up in the chair beside me with Agatha's paw draped across her leg, chuckled. "Those two could spot a Limoges plate in a dark alley."

At the word plate, Agatha leapt off her lap and trotted into the kitchen.

Doris continued, her voice rising just enough to be heard again. "You need to avoid the dishwasher with these, Gabby. The gilding's already fading on this one. Use a soft cloth and a gentle rinse."

"I always do," I called out, too tired to move but not too tired to defend my collection. "Even the chipped ones get treated like they're from Buckingham Palace."

"Oh, I like this one," Mabel chimed in again. "It's got a little blue cottage right in the center—looks like it belongs in a storybook."

"Or a murder mystery," Bernice murmured, grinning. Then she added, "Don't mind me. You two talk about whatever you need to talk about."

I didn't hesitate. "I'm sorry for judging your policing methods. By that, I mean being nice to Clarisa."

"I wasn't nice to her. I wanted to gauge her reaction to Dale being questioned so I fed her enough information to get a reaction."

"And did she have one?" Bernice asked.

"Not as much of one as I wanted."

Bernice set her knitting down on the table beside her. "What sort of reaction did you want?"

Sure, Bernice, don't mind you.

Brandon looked at me. "Grandview is Veronica's library right? So I thought maybe they would know what was going on in Veronica and Dale's life."

Bernice harrumphed. "Don't count on it. You are all spoiled by James's support of your library."

We both turned to her and waited.

"And…"

"Where is my cup of tea, Doris? I'm eighty-five, you know. I can't bustle around like I used to."

Oh so the eighty-five bullet could be used by any of them in any direction. I'd personally seen Bernice out-scramble a thirty year old.

"Here you go, in a Willowware tea cup. Don't break it."

"Don't drink out of that." I tried to heave myself off the couch, but my body wasn't cooperating. "That's not mine."

Brandon turned, already halfway to Bernice. "Is this from the Willowware set that was used for Veronica Steele's tea?"

"Yes," I said, heart thudding. "But I don't know how it got here. I gave all of it to the forensics team."

The room froze around us. Brandon sprang forward and snatched the cup from Bernice's hands.

Bernice's eyes widened like someone had told her they'd knit an entire sweater without dropping a stitch —or drinking coffee. "Someone snuck into your house and planted that cup?"

Doris, never far from a theory or a clean dish-towel, joined us, swinging the lemon-scented cloth over her shoulder. "With the state of her cabinets? Wouldn't be hard. They probably figured she'd never notice."

Thanks, Doris, for the vote of confidence in my house-keeping.

Brandon raised the cup to his nose, careful not to tip it. He inhaled slowly. "No scent. No residue. Just the faintest trace of black tea."

I watched him study the cup like it had just person-ally betrayed him—and maybe it had. The same borrowed tea set from Brett, the one we'd used at book club. The same set Veronica drank from before she collapsed.

"If someone used thallium or arsenic," he said

quietly, "you wouldn't smell a thing. That's what makes it effective—and dangerous."

He turned the cup slightly in his hands, examining it from all angles. "This wasn't meant to make a statement. It was meant to go unnoticed."

My stomach dropped. The room suddenly felt too bright, too sharp around the edges.

"Poison has a certain appeal," I said before I could stop myself.

Brandon looked over at me, brow raised.

"It has not the crudeness of the revolver bullet or the blunt weapon," I added, my voice softer now, like I was quoting from somewhere else. Because I was. "That's what Miss Marple said."

My eyes stayed fixed on the cup. It looked so ordinary. Innocent. Like something I'd cradle during a snowstorm while reading a cozy mystery—not something meant to end me.

"It's quiet," I whispered. "Subtle. You don't even know you're dying until it's already too late."

The silence that followed pressed in around me, heavy and tight. I wrapped my arms around myself, suddenly colder than I had any right to be.

"Someone left that for me," I said, heart thudding. "Not a warning. A weapon."

I looked from the teacup to Brandon, my brain trying to stitch sense from fear.

"Someone broke into my house," I said slowly, the words sounding strange out loud. "They put a teacup in my cabinet. Not just any cup—a vintage one, with a glaze made of poison. I mean, that's what I assume, based on every mystery novel I've ever read."

My throat tightened. "Why would someone want me dead?"

I shook my head, as if that could rattle the pieces into place. "And why tie it to Veronica Steele? What does her murder have to do with me?"

The silence that followed wasn't empty—it was heavy. As if even the air was waiting for the next chapter.

CHAPTER 16
WILLOWWARE WARS

"WE DON'T KNOW the Willowware tea cup was poisoned yet. So don't jump to conclusions," Brandon said as he slid the tea cup in a gallon baggie Doris had delivered to him.

Oh, I was jumping to conclusions as if I were an Olympic athlete with a pole vaulting gold metal.

"I'm going to take this into the station. Lock the doors. I'm going to ask Greg and Shane to sit outside your house and keep you safe.

"I'm sure she'd rather you stayed and kept her safe," Bernice said.

Brandon shut the door behind him without replying.

"I've got the table set," Mabel announced. "Let's eat."

Agatha was the first one in the dining room, where she sat sniffing the burger and fry-infused air.

"I'll get yours," Doris said to her. "But you don't get a fancy plate."

Agatha wagged her tail as if she understood. No fancy plate required. Just her burger patty and fries.

Once we were all seated at the table, I asked, "So what did you ladies find out today?"

"I thought you'd never ask," Bernice said as she squeezed a liberal amount of ketchup onto her floral plate.

I bit a mayo packet open with my mouth before asking, "What did you learn at The Daily Grind?"

Bernice stuffed a fry in her mouth. "You'll never guess who came in."

"Someone who had to do with the case!" Mabel added.

"Who?"

"The obsessed fan podcaster, Freda, and her boyfriend, Bert."

"What did she say?"

"She and Bert were talking about a new episode releasing tomorrow. She said it was called A Tribute To My Mother."

"What? Is she releasing a new podcast?"

The last time I'd talked to Freda and Bert they were both upset about the way Veronica had treated Freda. Bert was also upset at the fact their podcast and social media accounts were the reason Veronica's book sales took off.

"Has anyone looked at her social media accounts to see what the episode is really about?" I asked. Some titles were just clickbait.

"I don't do social media," Mabel said stoically.

"I don't know how to use those cell phone things. I still have a landline," Bernice added.

Doris chimed in, "I have a cell phone, but it is a flip phone."

"I'll grab my phone and check."

"It says here… No spoilers."

I continued reading, "But trust me, tomorrow's episode is the one I was *born* to record. The biggest reveal I've ever shared—and it changes *everything* you thought you knew about Veronica. You *do not* want to miss this."

"Bernice, you said you overheard her say A Tribute to My Mother. What does that mean? Veronica is her mother?"

Doris dabbed her lips with her napkin. "It's totally possible. Oh, I'm not supposed to tell anyone."

"You're not supposed to tell anyone what?"

"Veronica was pregnant and delivered a baby four years before her first bestseller."

"You mean James's book." I stood and grabbed a few empty plates and, while walking to the kitchen, added out loud, "That would make her sixteen at the time."

"So she wasn't married to Dale at the time. Do you think he knows?" I continued.

"We're still here, Miss Marple. You don't have to figure it all out by yourself."

"Oh, I'm not. This is how I process." I pushed off the couch and headed into the kitchen. From the fridge, I pulled out the pound cake I'd picked up at the bakery earlier in the week and set it on one of the plates Doris had polished. I left it on the counter and leaned through the opening into the dining room. "So you all knew Veronica when she was growing up?"

"I can't say we 'knew her.' Her father kept her up in that mansion he built on the edge of town. She didn't go to school."

"Yes, he had tutors for her and big plans of her taking over the business," Doris continued.

"Doris, you saw more of her than these two?"

"If you call doctor's appointments a couple times a year 'seeing her.'"

"You were her nurse?"

"Are we going to get any of that cake today?" Bernice asked, not interested in Doris's nursing career.

"Oh yes. Just a minute."

Agatha ran to the back door and yipped. She needed to go out and I had to take her. I wasn't letting one of the hens walk her in the dark only to fall and break a bone.

"Doris, can you serve the cake? I have to walk Agatha."

"Of course dear." She entered the kitchen with the lemon-scented hand towel on her shoulder. Did she carry that around in her dress pocket?

I slipped the harness on Agatha and tried to snap the leash on her while she jumped around like a toddler about to pee her pants.

"Hold still."

I picked her up and finally clicked the lead into place. I needn't worry about the hens. They could entertain themselves. Bernice and Mabel were already arguing about whether or not Veronica could be Freda's mother.

Once in the backyard, I pulled my phone out of my pocket while Agatha dragged me around the yard in pursuit of her nemesis, a gray squirrel. I guess researching Freda and Veronica would have to wait.

"You said you have to pee," I complained to Agatha. I stopped and put my hands on my knees. Breathing through my nose was not an option. I guessed it was time to take a page from Doris's book—and actually follow her medical advice.

The gray squirrel skittered up the base of an oak tree to a branch high enough to be safe from Agatha's kangaroo hops and turned around to bark back at her.

With the squirrel out of play, surely Agatha would do her business. Nope. She heard something at the front of the house and tore off in the direction of the front yard.

We rounded the corner only to hear Officer Shane yell, "Put your hands in the air."

Agatha disregarded the command and strained at the edge of her leash and growled.

"Shane, it's me. The person you're supposed to be protecting."

"Get back inside. It's not safe out here."

I looked up and down the quiet street, leaves falling in slow motion in the glowing street lamps. Not a person or animal in sight.

"Looks safe to me," I said to Officer Shane.

"It's always calmest before the storm."

My neighbor, Miranda, stuck her head out her front door, wearing her signature evening attire - satin robe and pjs."Hey Gabby, I'm so glad…"

I stepped under the street light.

"Oh my gosh. Look at your face. No wonder you have police protection."

This is the point that most people say "you should have seen the other guy." Except the "other guy" was a girl six inches shorter than me with muscles that belonged to a body builder and she didn't have a scratch on her.

"I'm so glad I saw the fight at the town square and called Brittany."

"You saw it?"

"My whole office did. When you ran out of the library after those two ladies, Germaine told us all to stop what we were doing and come and watch."

Great. Everyone saw Clarisa kill my face.

My front door opened and Bernice leaned out, brandishing a knitting needle like a weapon. "Whoever is out there… I'm armed."

"I'm okay, Bernice. I'm just talking to my neighbor."

"Well, invite her in!" Mabel shouted through the window she'd just opened.

These ladies had no idea what police protection meant. Of course neither did the officers guarding me. Hadn't they just treated me as if I were an intruder in my own yard?

Then I had a thought. "Miranda, didn't you grow up in Grandview?"

"Yes, I did."

Bernice had stepped out on the front porch. She wagged a knitting needle at Miranda. "Why don't you come over and have some pound cake, dearie? You look like you could use the calories."

Once Miranda was seated at the table, Doris served her a generous slice of pound cake with whipped cream and strawberries. I didn't even know I had whipped cream and strawberries in my fridge.

"I know what this is about," Miranda said as she sliced a paper thin sliver of cake. "You want to know why I didn't come to book club Monday when Veronica Steele did her reading. I love book club. I do. I did not like Veronica..." She scooped up the sliver and daintily slid it in her mouth.

"Did you know her?"

"Everyone in Grandview knew of her."

"But you knew her," I pressed.

"I did until she dropped off the face of the earth."

"Explain," Bernice said, leaning in with both of her hands wrapped around a tea cup.

"Well, I wasn't from a wealthy family like she was. Let's just say I wasn't on her approved list of friends."

She leaned back in her chair and shut her eyes as if trying to conjure up a memory.

"But she used to sneak out and come to my house. We got along pretty well until..."

"She got pregnant," Doris said in her matter-of-fact nurse voice.

"I suspected, but I didn't know for sure. All I knew was she disappeared."

"Did you ever see her again?"

"You mean did we remain friends and play board games at my house with my mom and dad? No. When I was seventeen I went to college."

"And when you returned, she was a bestselling author."

"Yes, and it made me angry. She never called or reached out or anything."

"So you waited twenty years, showed up to the book reading and poisoned her, slipping out before anyone saw you."

"Stop it Bernice, you are not Poirot. Or Miss Marple. This is Gabby's friend," Mabel chided.

"Next thing you know, you're going to be reminding me I'm eighty-five."

Miranda popped a strawberry in her mouth and then chuckled. "No, I did not murder Veronica. And although she hurt me because we were friends, I didn't want her dead."

"Why settle here instead of Grandview?" I asked.

"Good question. I wanted to build something of my own. I wanted to be a big fish in a small pond. I couldn't do that in Grandview."

Miranda had built a thriving real estate business and had a reputation of being the best.

"Plus I have great friends." She smiled at me. "Gabby keeps this town interesting."

By "keeps this town interesting," she meant dead bodies seemed to show up around me and someone or other was always trying to murder me.

Miranda stood. "I've got some files to go through. Thanks for the cake."

"One more question. Do you know who Freda, host of True Crime Lovers Podcast is?"

"Yes, I've heard of her. Her social media says she has some life-changing announcement tomorrow morning."

"Do you listen to her?"

"No, but I will tomorrow."

"Thanks, goodnight."

The hens all clucked their versions of "goodnight."

"Take some pound cake to go… you need it."

"Have one of those nice officers walk you home."

"Text Gabby when you get there."

Now I needed the hens to leave so I could do some research and go to bed. Their ride, Detective Brandon, had left. I didn't think I could get officer Shane to leave his post. The hens didn't look as if they were ready to go. Doris and Mabel moved to the kitchen and started washing and putting away dishes. Bernice settled back in the chair in the living room with her knitting.

I slipped into the bathroom with my phone and called Brittany. I'd bribe her with the information on Veronica possibly being Freda's mother and the murder attempt on my life in exchange for her taking the hens to their Airbnb.

"Hey Brittany!" I said as she answered the phone.

"Why are you calling instead of texting me? What's wrong?"

"Someone tried to murder me tonight." I left off the word allegedly. If she could play with words, so could I.

"I'll be over there in ten minutes."

No need to bribe her then.

Ten minutes later, she stormed through the door, brandishing a can of mace.

Bernice screamed and dropped her knitting.

"I meant earlier," I explained, while Agatha ran around her legs and stopped to lick her shoes.

"You made it sound as if you were in trouble."

"We took care of her." Bernice leaned over to pick up her knitting needles and mass of moss green yarn.

Brittany slid the mace back in her pocket.

"Didn't the police stop you?" I asked, while pulling back the curtain to check on Greg and Shane.

"They're watching Rookie on a tablet. They didn't even notice me." She glanced around the living room. "I thought Detective Brandon would be here."

"He was earlier. He took the possibly poisoned tea cup to the station."

"What?"

I explained the whole "someone snuck in my house and left a Willowware poison teacup" theory.

"Wow. Why does someone want you dead?"

"I asked the same question."

"Because she is going to figure out who murdered Veronica," Doris said as she joined her on the couch. "Don't suppose we could bother you for a ride to our Airbnb?"

"Doris, why don't you tell Brittany about Veronica having a baby when she was sixteen"

Brittany shot up off the couch. "What? You couldn't have told me that on the phone?"

"I thought my potential death was more important."

"Not to…" she stopped herself. "I mean, of course, but this is *news*."

So my potential death wasn't *news*. Just another day in the life of a mystery-loving Miss Marple fan librarian. Broken nose. Poison. But not enough danger to warrant a headline.

"Someone beat you to the punch," Mabel said as she entered the room, drying her hands on the lemon dishtowel.

"What?" Brittany pulled her phone out and scrolled on social media.

"Look at Freda's True Crime Lovers account," I offered.

Brittany scrolled and paced. "Son of a buttered biscuit."

She paused and turned to the hens. "I'll take you to your Airbnb if you can be in the car in two minutes."

Bernice stuffed her knitting in her bag. "I'm ready now."

"Where are you going?" I asked, suddenly feeling left out and less like I wanted them to leave so I could be alone.

Brittany stopped with her hand on the doorknob. "To talk to Freda, of course."

CHAPTER 17
POLICE PROTECTION SLEEP OVER?

"I WANT TO COME."

"Don't you think you should stay home because of..." Brittany pointed at my face.

"Yes, dear," Doris added. "You need to rest and remember all my instructions."

I knew they were right, but I didn't want to be left out of the interview. They clucked all the way out the door, asking Brittany questions.

"Isn't this exciting?" Bernice said, her voice trailing off as she descended the porch steps. "This week was well worth the one hundred..."

After they left, I sat down on the couch and clutched a pillow to my chest. Okay. Enough feeling sorry for myself. Time to get to work.

I grabbed my laptop and set up at the dining room table. Time to do some research. I could send what I found to Brittany so she'd have some ammunition for her questions.

First off, to find Freda's birth date. Easy enough. It was on her social media. She was twenty-four. Veronica gave birth at sixteen. Did the numbers add up? They did.

Freda was born at Grandview Memorial Hospital. I didn't have access to the adoption records, or a hacker to access them for me. But I could find out the names of her parents. They were listed and linked on her social media. Maybe Brittany could contact them and confirm Freda's theory.

I sent the names — Harold and Marjorie — via text and continued to research. After exhausting all I could cover from my end, I had a thought. Hadn't Veronica said she had a new book releasing soon? Maybe I could find it on Goodreads if it was set up for pre-order. That's right…it was the upcoming release she had done a reading from, *Twenty Years Gone: A Stolen Past. A Reckoning Ahead.*

On Veronica's Author Page, I found the book.

I adjusted my glasses and stared at the screen, the cover of *Twenty Years Gone* staring right back like it knew something I didn't. Veronica Steele's final novel—scheduled for release a full year after her murder. That alone was enough to make my investigator's heart twitch. But it was the title that sent the real shiver: *Twenty Years Gone: A Stolen Past. A Reckoning Ahead.*

It didn't feel like fiction.

The hospital bracelet on the cover bore the name *Lila.* Not a common placeholder name like "Jane" or "Emily."

And now Freda, Veronica's Steele's number one fan

and podcast queen, is teasing "the biggest news of her life" on tomorrow's episode—and I have a sinking suspicion I already know what she's going to say.

She thinks Veronica was her mother.

I leaned closer to the screen. If this book is Veronica's final message, it might not just be about a character's lost identity—it could be Veronica telling the truth the only way she knew how: on the page.

Which means this isn't just research.

Someone is trying to tell the truth.

It's evidence.

Twenty Years Gone
A Baby Disappears. A Woman Returns.
At twenty-two, she believed she had nothing to hide —until she discovered the file in a closet: a birth certificate, a hospital bracelet, a single line in a cold case report. That evidence proved she wasn't who she thought she was. Someone stole her past, and now, she's determined to reclaim it.
Driven by a name she's never known and a family she's never met, she leaves everything behind. With every lead she uncovers—from police timelines to a stranger's whispered confession—she finds herself stalking an invisible trail of secrets. But as she closes in, she realizes the deeper danger isn't that someone took her—it's that someone might still want to keep her hidden.
For fans of *The Nowhere Child* and *True Identity, Twenty Years Gone* pulls you into the fractured heart of identity, the unbearable weight of unanswered

**questions, and a daughter's fight to unearth the truth
that's been buried for two decades.**

There was something else I couldn't shake. If Owen
and I were correct in our theory that Veronica Steele
never wrote a book, only stole them from her protégés,
who wrote this one? Freda wasn't a writer and if she
had written the book, she wouldn't have waited this
long to tell the truth about Veronica being her mother.

The computer screen swam in front of my eyes. I
removed my glasses, giving the bridge of my nose a
break from the weight of them. The meds I had taken
after Brittany and the hens had left was making me feel
loopy again. I closed the laptop and stood and
stretched.

"Ready to go out one last time before I fall asleep?" I
asked Agatha, who was already sleeping peacefully on
the floor.

I picked her up by her middle and she hung like a
rag doll.

I carried her to the back door and slid her harness on
and clicked it into place. "I don't care if you want to
sleep. You can pee first."

Once I set her on the frosty ground, it was as if I had
flipped a switch. She pranced across the frozen leaves,
trying to avoid the ice crystals. She stopped under the
maple tree to pee before zipping to the back door like a
bullet train.

Once inside, I wiped her paws with the tea towel
hanging on a hook by the back door. The storm door
clicked shut. Before I closed the main door, I caught a
glimpse of a shadowy figure in the yard. I quickly

slammed the door and grabbed my phone to call Shane, who was probably still watching The Rookie with Greg and paying no attention to the murderer lurking in my backyard.

Before I could unlock my phone, someone pounded on the back door. I jumped ten feet in the air—figuratively—and landed hard enough that the jolt rattled through my already-broken nose. The pain zinged straight to my eyes, and for a moment, I saw actual sparkles. Not the magical kind.

"Gabby, it is Brandon. Let me in."

I opened the door. "You scared the life out of me."

"You shouldn't be walking Agatha alone in the dark."

"She had to pee."

"I'll take her next time."

"So I'm supposed to text you in the middle of the night if she has to go?"

"You won't have to. I'm staying the night."

"Greg and Shane are here."

"No, I sent them home. Let's just say, I don't trust them with your safety. I walked right by them and they didn't notice."

"Let me guess. They were watching The Rookie."

"How did you know?"

"Brittany was here a little over an hour ago and they were watching it then. They didn't even notice her."

It was in that moment that the *I'm staying the night* comment finally sank in.

This was *not* how I'd imagined our first night together as a couple.

Me with a broken nose, drugged up on painkillers,

and someone trying to kill me with a poisoned teacup? Hardly romantic.

Nope. I'd imagined this night plenty of times, thank you very much. In every scenario, it started with a wedding. A sweet, small-town wedding on my back lawn. Brittany and her mom would be there. Her mom, Sally, of course would bake the cake. A triple-layer almond with raspberry filling and vanilla buttercream roses. I'd wear the vintage white lace dress I'd found at Second Hand Chic last spring and promptly hid in the back of my closet after that ill-fated, two-sips-of-wine-induced proposal. He hadn't said no. That had to count for something.

"You're looking kind of flushed, Gabby. You should go to bed."

When he said "bed", *his* face flushed the color of a sugar maple in October—bold, bright, and trying valiantly not to be obvious about it.

I wrapped my arms around my waist, self-conscious. "You don't have to sleep on the couch."

"What?"

"I mean—I have a spare bedroom. It's not like those mysteries we watch where the guest always sleeps on the couch even though the house has twenty bedrooms." I could hear the words leaving my mouth and wished I had a rewind button. "I wasn't inviting you to *my* bed. I mean, obviously. Because we're not doing *that* until we're married. And you didn't say no, you know."

Brandon chuckled—the low, warm kind that made me wish I didn't have a swollen face and an ice pack slowly melting against my cheek. "You're right," he said, straightening with a smile that was half amusement, half something more. He tucked both hands into his jean pockets. "But I think you've had enough of whatever the hospital gave you. Let's get you to bed—your bed. Alone. I'll take the guest room."

I pointed a finger at him. "Good. Because I meant it."

"I know you did."

And somehow, the air between us held the kind of unspoken promise that had nothing to do with spare bedrooms or poisoned teacups, and everything to do with the long game. Cozy, complicated, and possibly forever.

———

"What are you doing?" Brandon asked as he entered the dining room, looking super handsome despite a case of bedhead.

It was six fifty-nine and I'd already walked Rory and made coffee. How did I answer him in less than a minute? Freda's podcast dropped at seven a.m. I didn't want to miss Freda's big announcement.

"Waiting for True Crime Lovers Podcast to drop. There's coffee in the kitchen."

"Good morning to you too." Brandon smiled and ran his hands through his hair with a yawn, headed to the kitchen without another word.

The doorbell chimed. "Yohoo, we're here!"

Oh great. The hens were here. Why were they here? How did they get here?

"No need to ring the doorbell. I practically live

here." Brittany jiggled the door handle. "Gabby, let us in. We're going to miss the podcast."

"We brought breakfast," Bernice added.

"Hope you made coffee."

What did I do? Hide Brandon in the closet? Push him out the back door and toss his clothes after him? No. That sounded bad. It wasn't like he wasn't dressed —he was. In a soft, well-worn T-shirt that clung in all the right places and a pair of gray joggers that looked one wash away from retirement. Casual, comfortable, and maddeningly good-looking in that just-rolled-out-of-bed-with-coffee sort of way.

I had no chance to make a decision, let alone a plan, because Brandon, coffee in hand, answered the door.

"Good morning ladies. We're all set up in the dining room to listen to the podcast."

I hoped the swelling and discoloration on my face covered the red that was climbing up my neck and turning me into a tomato.

I didn't get the chance to see the looks on their faces at Brandon opening the door. But I heard the gasps and the "oh my"s and the one "you go girl", which I'm positive was Bernice's voice.

"Don't get too excited. Nothing happened. I know —" Mabel stopped herself as the intro to the podcast played. I turned it up.

"Hey fellow crime lovers and Veronica Steele fans. As you know, I had to deliver some bad news the other day. True legend and crime fiction genius was murdered. We're still grieving here. But today's big reveal will change everything. Hang on to your seats, listeners. You're not going to want to miss this. I'll be right back after a word from our sponsor."

🎙️ *[Upbeat music plays softly in the background]*
"This episode of True Crime Lovers Podcast is brought to you by **Whodunit Wonders Candle Co.,** the only candle line inspired by classic mysteries and modern sleuths alike.

Need to calm your nerves after a murder plot twist? Try *Miss Marple's Garden*—it smells like lavender, fresh tea leaves, and a hint of suspicion. Or light up *Hard-Boiled Alibi*, with rich tobacco, leather-bound books, and danger lurking in the shadows.

Visit **WhodunitWonders.com** and use code **STEELE20** for 20% off your first order. Because nothing says 'Murder Mystery Vibes' like a murder-themed candle."
🎙️ *[Music fades out]*

As the hens set out biscuits and gravy, making themselves at home in my kitchen, pulling out plates and mugs, we waited.

Before the music ended, the doorbell chimed again.

"Gabby, it's Dale. I need to talk to you and Detective Brandon."

Brandon opened the door again.

Did the whole town know Brandon spent the night, including the Grandview visitors? My reputation was shot. Wait. Why was I worrying about my reputation? I'd already been arrested for murder once. I think that counts for ruining my reputation.

"Someone stole Veronica's manuscript," Dale blurted before stepping inside.

That's karma, right? She'd been allegedly stealing manuscripts for years and calling them her own. Now she's dead and someone decided to get even. In the background the podcast played and, as I joined Brandon at the door, we heard Freda bragging, "I've read Veronica's newest manuscript."

"I think I know who stole the manuscript."

"You do?" Dale asked.

"Did you by any chance let Freda interview you for the podcast True Crime Lovers Podcast?"

"Yes, but I have a standard set of questions and answers approved by the publisher. I didn't tell her anything about the new book you couldn't find online."

"Where did she interview you?"

"My hotel room. Her boyfriend, Bert, set up all this fancy equipment."

"Bingo."

Freda went on and on about the book. She had more information than the Goodreads blurb, or she inferred more about the book.

I turned to Brittany who was hunched over my laptop listening to the podcast. "Turn it up, please."

She did just in time for the hens to come in the dining room clucking and setting down plates of biscuits and gravy.

They were loud but not loud enough to block us from hearing.

"So listeners, it is evident that Veronica, my mother, wrote this book about me. I'm the baby in Twenty Years Gone."

Dale took the ten steps it took to get in the dining room. "I didn't tell her that."

"You mean it's true?" Brittany asked, not missing a beat.

"I don't know. That's one of the reasons I was having Veronica ruled incompetent. She'd been going on and on about a baby and making restitution with people she'd wronged. And she was sending people money. Our account was draining like a sieve."

It was my turn to ask a question. "Did you know that your wife stole manuscripts from her protégées?"

His face turned ashen. And for the third time since he'd entered my house this morning, he said, "What?"

Doris pulled out a chair for him. "Sit, dear, drink some coffee. I'll grab some extra sugar."

The podcast droned on in the background, Freda giving more than one spoiler. All eyes were on Dale. I sat down and Doris came in with the sugar cubes and dumped enough in to sweeten a cake. She offered him a spoon and he stirred it with a vacant look on his face.

Mabel served up a plate of biscuits and gravy and shoved it toward him. "Eat up."

He picked up the mug and took a large swig before stirring it. Dale mechanically picked up the fork and shoved a bite in his mouth, his meaty jowls and beefy arms trembling.

After he swallowed a few bites, he stopped with the fork in midair. "I've never read any of Veronica's books."

It was our turn, as a group, to say, "What?"

"You have to understand. I kept the books. I played golf at the country club…"

"What did Veronica do?"

"She stayed holed up in the mansion her dad left her, writing."

"Except she wasn't writing," Brittany said.

"I guess there are a lot of things I didn't know about her."

"If I may be bold," Bernice said from the other end of the table where she had seated herself with her knitting like Miss Marple. "Why did you marry her?"

Dale didn't look stunned this time. He looked ashamed. "When her dad got sick ten years ago, he asked me to manage her finances and watch over her."

"He paid you to marry her, huh?" Bernice asked, not missing a beat.

"Yes, I was given a certain allowance. We weren't a traditional couple."

"So you didn't consummate the marriage?" Bernice challenged.

"You can't ask him that," Mabel said.

"I'm eighty-five, as you two like to remind me often. I can ask whatever I want."

Dale answered quietly. "No, like I said, we were married in name only."

"Then she went off the rails, spending money and writing a new will."

"She had always been a lot to handle, but these last few months..." he trailed off.

I didn't feel sorry for Dale. He'd married a woman, likely twenty years younger than him, for her money, status, and country club golf games and lunches. When Veronica started spending too much of her money, he filed to have her declared incompetent so he could take over the entire estate. He was a leech and, as far as I was concerned, a criminal.

Dale took a few more bites as we listened to the end of the podcast.

He wiped his mouth on one of my daisy-patterned cloth napkins and stood. I had the sudden urge to toss the napkin straight in the trash—I was that disgusted.

"So are you going to get the manuscript back? It's worth a lot of money," Dale demanded.

"Well that depends," Brandon said, standing and placing his hands on hips like he did while in uniform. Except he was in an old tee and sweats and his hair was standing on ends. I wanted to laugh. "If Freda is biologically her daughter, that may be something for the courts to decide." I wanted to hug him.

Dale threw my napkin on the plate where it soaked up the greasy sausage residue, likely ruining it.

Doris reached over his shoulder and rescued it. "I'll go get this soaking with a little baking soda."

"Young man, I think it's time you left." Bernice commanded without looking up from her knitting.

Dale stormed out the front door, Agatha barking at his heels.

The door slammed behind him and then we enjoyed the rest of our breakfast while Brittany started to fill us in on what she found out from Freda.

"She stonewalled me. 'Listen to the podcast' is all she would say."

"But we filled Brittany in on all we learned yesterday," Mabel offered.

Brittany stood and swung her leather satchel over her shoulder. "Now I have to go write an article."

I smoothed my hair. "And I've got to get to work."

"Me too."

"We'll clean up," Doris offered, "while you get ready."

Bernice set her knitting on the table. "Are The Sleuths meeting today?"

"Yes," I answered, and then I had a thought. "How would you ladies like to help with story hour?"

CHAPTER 18
HENS AT STORY HOUR

THE LIBRARY WAS BUSTLING with regulars again—whether because the crime scene tape was finally gone or simply because people missed their books. Honestly, I doubted most of them cared that a famous author had died here. What mattered was that story hour had been canceled and moms had been without a library for a few days. That was punishment enough. All those dramatic promises about never stepping foot in here until the murder was solved? Forgotten.

Allison stopped just inside the door and gave me a once-over. "Oh honey," she said, her eyes landing on my nose. "That looks painful."

"Just got in the way of an elbow," I said casually. "Nothing dramatic."

Evie peeked out from behind her legs and pointed. "Boo-boo nose," she announced.

"Yes, sweetie," Allison said, lifting her onto one hip. "But Miss Gabby's still here and still smiling."

Ned gasped when he saw me. "Whoa! Did you get that in *Super Mario Wonder*? Like—were you fighting Piranha Plants or riding the wiggly pipes?"

"Nothing quite that exciting," I said, giving him a small smile. "Just real life being clumsy."

He nodded, serious. "You need a Wonder Flower. Those fix everything."

Agatha greeted the story hour kids, tail wagging, as Ned took the lead. "Hey Agatha. Want to play Super Mario Wonder?" he called, dashing around the table with her yipping at his heels.

"No more Sasquatch?" I asked, remembering last spring when Ned had marched in with a cooler, scribbled maps, and a plastic sausage taped to a stick. He'd worn a crayon-labeled "PARK RANGER" badge and had declared, "Sasquatch patrol! Last seen near the circulation desk—stealing snacks again!"

"No. I'm done with that game. Mario is my new favorite." He paused to take a breath and Agatha plowed into the back of his knees, throwing him off kilter. He caught himself on a table. "I'm five and a half now, Gabby," he added, as if that explained everything.

"By that he means he's obsessed," Allison added, dumping a diaper bag on the table with a sigh.

Story hour felt extra fall-ish that morning thanks to the pumpkin garlands strung across the windows and the faint scent of cinnamon wafting from Bernice's tote bag. She swore it was her yarn, but I suspected otherwise. I'd stacked a display of squirrel-themed picture books by the beanbag chairs for Bernice to choose from.

She settled into the rocking chair with *Miss Suzy* in hand—an old favorite about a squirrel who loses her treehouse and enlists a group of toy soldiers to take it back. The cover was worn soft from decades of page-turning. A classic, just like Bernice.

Ned plopped down front and center, his red shirt practically glowing under his overalls, his homemade "MARIO" badge now sporting a smiley face sticker. "Is this the one where the squirrel builds a secret fort in the attic?" he whispered loudly to Agatha, who was already dozing at his feet.

"You'll see," I said, sliding onto a seat next to Mabel and Doris, who were already sipping fresh coffee from the machine James Hatterson donated to the fishbowl room. Doris took a thoughtful sip, then nodded at the book in Bernice's hands. "Bernice might be eighty-five, but she picked the right one. Original publication date was 1950. That generation knew how to spot a classic."

I bit back a smile. Doris had been born not long after 1950 herself, which probably explained her unshakable belief that her era got most things right, including children's books.

Bernice opened the book, her voice smooth and sure. "In the tip-tip-top of a tall oak tree lived Miss Suzy…"

Ned gasped. "She lives in a tree?! That's like Flower Kingdom—only cozier. And less musical pipes."

Mabel leaned toward me. "Is he always this… spirited?"

"Last spring he was on Sasquatch patrol," I whispered. "He taped a plastic sausage to a stick and claimed the culprit was hiding behind the nonfiction shelves."

Doris chuckled. "At least he's seasonal."

When the red squirrels stormed Miss Suzy's home,

Ned leaned forward like it was a full-blown heist. "This is AWESOME! Do the talking flowers warn her first?"

"No flowers," Bernice said, not missing a beat. "But she does make a cozy new house in the attic."

He nodded solemnly. "Smart. Like Drill Mario—go underground, rebuild, and come back stronger."

Bernice raised an eyebrow at me, the yellow hardback copy resting in her lap. "Is that a compliment?"

"From Ned? That's high praise."

By the time the toy soldiers helped Miss Suzy reclaim her treehouse, half the kids were sprawled across the rug in a happy tangle of limbs and crayons. Agatha had joined them. And Mabel had dozed off, her head tilted just so.

"The end," Bernice read, closing the book with a satisfied thump.

Ned jumped up and saluted. "That was awesome. Miss Suzy's got backup. And snacks. She's like—squirrel Mario!"

I smiled and collected the book from Bernice. "Not bad for a Thursday, huh?"

She just winked and said, "Even squirrels need their quiet places. Just like librarians."

Allison and Mary had prepped the snacks—protein mini pumpkin muffins and apple cider. Today felt like a heavenly slice of normal.

For a fleeting moment, I let myself breathe. No one had mentioned the murder yet, and I was quietly thankful. It was as if I could shelve it—gently, like a rare book with a cracked spine—just for an hour or so, before The Sleuths arrived and we cracked the cover open again. I needed that pause, the illusion of peace, even if it was paper-thin.

Still, the questions lingered like the scent of cinnamon in the air. Did Freda kill Veronica? Did she resent Veronica for giving her up for adoption, if that was true, of course? Or was Dale my prime suspect after his early morning breakfast admission? Marrying Veronica for her money and bleeding her bank account dry with his country club tab wasn't exactly a declaration of innocence. And who casually admits that over free sausage and biscuits made by the hens?

I sipped my cider, letting the tart warmth ground me. I wasn't solving anything just yet. For now, there were muffins. And a moment's quiet.

The story hour moms packed up and left with a great many thanks to the hens and a few instructions to how to care for my broken nose.

Doris quipped, "Now don't you young moms worry. Nurse Doris will take care of her."

After a few minutes, Allison re-entered the library sans children. "I hope you don't mind. I'd like to attend The Sleuths meeting. I assume you are working on the murder case." She whispered the word murder as if her kids were still present. I peered out the front windows looking for them.

"My husband has the day off," she said in explanation. "He is taking them to the park and then The Tasty Burger for lunch so I'm free til nap time. He can't handle that." Then she murmured to herself, "All you have to do is read a story, get them a drink and…sorry did i say that out loud?"

"I'm happy you can stay!"I responded. "You can

help me make some fresh coffee. Mary went to buy some donuts and walk Agatha."

As we set up the coffee, The Sleuths began to arrive. First James, looking his chipper and debonair self, followed by Randolph, Thomas, Antonio, and…who was that with Emory? Emily.

"Hope you don't mind that I brought a date!" Emory yelled across the library.

First of all, yelling in libraries is a no-no unless you're a story hour kiddo. And second of all, no, you do not bring a date to The Sleuths, especially when we are not working a fictional crime. Then again, Emory had no social skills. So I figured I'd give him some grace, not to mention, I was happy he had someone new to crush on.

I didn't answer him because that would require yelling across the library. I waited until The Sleuths congregated in the fishbowl room before asking, "Where is Owen?"

"Do we need him to start?" Antonio asked.

"Yeah, we do. He has pretty much done most of the research."

It was getting stuffy in the fishbowl room with all these bodies. I felt like a fish with no water—trapped behind glass and gulping air. "I'm going to grab my coffee and we can set up in the back conference room." Definitely not our norm, but with this many people and the kind of research we were doing, being out of sight and earshot of the patrons was a great idea.

Not to mention the fact that after last spring's near-death incident in this very room, I didn't like it as much anymore. The glass felt more like a cage than a window.

Too many memories pressed in with the smudges on the panes. I'd smiled through it, of course. Told myself it was just a room. But even now, my shoulders tightened as I turned the knob, ready to escape its walls and the ghosts they held.

I exited the fishbowl room and walked down the narrow hallway to the conference room. Emily followed.

"I hope you don't mind I came along with Emory."

"No, not at all," my mouth replied automatically, while my brain threw its hands in the air. Why in the world would she spend her hard-earned money on a hotel to stay another night in Maplewood instead of heading back to Grandview? And—no offense—why Emory?

I mean, Emory Finch wasn't exactly the type who turned heads. Unless it was in mild confusion. He had that long, lanky frame that moved like a heron trying to navigate a crowded dock. His small wire-rimmed glasses perpetually threatened to leap off his nose like they, too, were unsure about his life choices. He always looked slightly startled, as if someone had tapped him on the shoulder in the middle of a nap.

Don't get me wrong—he was nice. Smart, too, in a forgot-to-comb-his-hair-because-he-was-reading-a-forensics-journal sort of way. But romance? With Emory? My brain couldn't file that under anything other than "unusual library acquisitions."

"It's just that Emory said you had a crush on him. Like you couldn't decide between him and Detective Brandon."

I nearly tripped over my own feet.

A *crush* on *Emory*? My mouth opened, then closed again, like a goldfish realizing it was in the wrong tank.

I mean, sure—he was kind in a jittery, academic sort of way. But if Emory was a bird, he'd be a distracted stork caught in a wind tunnel. Sweet, harmless, and often mistaken for part of the background decor.

Detective Brandon Hale, on the other hand—well, he didn't blend into anything. The first time I met him, he stepped out of the shadows like a plot twist in a well-paced mystery, his presence quietly commanding the space without a single word. At 6'1" in a crisp shirt and tailored slacks, he looked like he belonged in the sort of suspense novel you dog-ear and reread. Steel-gray eyes that didn't just see you—they dissected you. And that faint five o'clock shadow? It hinted at something rugged beneath all that polish, like he could quote policy *and* fix a broken fence.

Brandon was a locked-room mystery you wanted to solve. Emory… was the footnote in a textbook about forensic fungi.

If Emory thought I was torn between the two of them, he'd clearly mistaken a glance for longing. I needed to start shelving his self-confidence under "fantasy."

And maybe I should've seen this coming. After all, during the last case, Emory all but declared he cracked it single-handedly—told us it wasn't some big Sherlock moment, but how he'd stopped thinking like an investigator and started thinking like the killer. That every murder had followed an Agatha Christie plot…until it didn't.

CHAPTER 19
HENS, SLEUTHS, AND THE FORGOTTEN CHILD

TO END my uncomfortable conversation about Emory with Emily in the hallway, I assured her I'd chosen Detective Brandon.

She uncrossed her arms and they relaxed against her sides.

"Oh, good."

I unlocked the conference room and she turned to rejoin Emory, I assumed. "Good luck," I called after her.

"I don't think I need it."

What did she mean by that? With me out of the way, she was sure to nab her man? Now I sounded like a 1950s Tommy and Tuppence novel in my head. Maybe Bernice had rubbed off on me. I was going to miss her and the other hens when they went home to Grandview.

A notification pinged on my phone. An email from the State Library Commission with the subject line:

Appointment Opportunity: Head Librarian – Grandview Public Library
Dear Ms. Keats,
On behalf of the State Library Commission, I am writing to formally invite you to consider the recently vacated position of Head Librarian at Grandview Public Library. Your exemplary service in Maplewood has not gone unnoticed, and we believe you would be an outstanding fit for this leadership role.

What? I couldn't believe it. After all the snide remarks. Angela had gone on about her superior library and my little wanna-be version, but this—well, this was more than what those in the murder mystery genre might call simple revenge. To me, it was proof that I did matter. I was doing a good job and someone noticed. I'd waited for approval like this my whole life, ever since the years in foster care when I was told I was never good enough.

I started a list on my notes app as if I'd already accepted the position.

- Contact Miranda and put the house on the market.
- Look for a house in Grandview – who was a I kidding, I'd be lucky to afford a small apartment there. But wait, I'm sure there was a pay increase.
- Let staff know I'm leaving.
- Let The Sleuths know I'm leaving
- Break it off with Brandon

"Oh hey, Gabby." Mary stepped in the room with a white bakery box and Agatha bobbing her head in excitement behind her.

I set my phone down quickly. Screen side down.

"Oh. Did you get some bad news?"

I took the box and set it in the middle of the table.

"No. Good news. A job offer." Pretty sure I was breaking the tell-your-best-friend-first rule. Or was it supposed to be the boyfriend you proposed to first?

"Oh." She looked disappointed. "But who would run the library here? And the book club, The Sleuths…"

James entered back first, carrying a tray with a carafe of coffee and assorted mugs.

I put my finger to my lips and whispered, "I haven't told anyone yet."

Anyone but her. Brittany already had a job in Grandview so maybe it was time for her to move there too.

Before I could give the job and move another moment's thought, the rest of The Sleuths entered, Emily hanging on Emory's bony elbow. Allison and Owen brought up the rear with the murder board in tow. The murder board-turned-"who had Veronica stolen manuscripts from" board.

I wanted to find out what Owen had learned, but that wasn't the first item on our agenda. First, the True Crime Lovers Podcast.

Owen grabbed a cinnamon twist and cleared his throat.

He wrapped it in a napkin like a burrito. "Should we start with the obvious question?"

"Is Veronica Freda's mother?" James asked, leading the way.

I scanned The Sleuths, looking for clues on their faces. My eyes landed briefly on Emily. She was studying the board pretty intently for a newbie. "How about we turn this board over?"

Allison raised her hand and offered, "You mean start a timeline for Veronica's life and see what we can find?"

Thomas stood and flipped the board over on the easel. "Yes."

He wrote "Veronica Steele" on top of the board.

"We could listen to the podcast again and write down the facts Freda said," Antonio suggested.

"We have to assume," I said, adjusting my glasses, "that not everything Freda says is, well, fact-checked."

James raised an eyebrow. "You think she's lying?"

"Not lying, exactly," I replied, tapping the marker on my chin. "Let's just say, believing everything you hear in a podcast is a dangerous habit. I gave up trusting well-packaged stories a long time ago."

Antonio frowned. "But she sounded so sure. Like she knew everything."

I gave a small nod. "Miss Marple once said it's dangerous to believe everything people tell you. She never trusted anyone's word at face value."

Bernice chuckled from her chair, knitting needles clicking. "That's from Sleeping Murder, isn't it, sugar?"

"Exactly."

Bernice grinned. "Good girl. Never trust a voice just 'cause it's got good teeth and a microphone."

"All right then," Thomas said, standing with a dry-erase marker. "Let's get back to it. Timeline starts now."

Agatha scuttled under the table looking for donut crumbs while the rest of us scoured the internet for facts about Veronica. The hens relied on their memories instead of Google. Let's just say their memories disagreed with each other. In the end, we had to give Doris' account of Veronica's early life the most credit because she was the family's nurse.

Brittany swept into the room in a huff, slung her backpack onto the table, and popped open the pastry box like it had personally wronged her. She plucked a pumpkin cake donut with chocolate chips, took a bite, and pointed dramatically. "You are not going to believe who I just talked to."

Mid-chew, she caught sight of the board and paused. "Doris is right. Veronica had a baby."

"Well, of course I'm right," Doris huffed.

I jumped in before things spiraled into a full-on bake sale debate. "Who did you talk to?"

"I talked to Veronica's old tutor — Nigel Fair-weather."

Thomas added his name to the board.

"How many years was he her tutor?"

"From kindergarten to graduation."

"Yes, I remember that name," James added. He paused to sip his coffee. "It was he who contacted me about mentoring her."

Antonio chuckled. "She had a tutor at the age of twenty?I thought it took me a long time to graduate high school. At least I finished when I was nineteen."

I didn't want anyone to say anything mean to Antonio. He wasn't the brightest banana in the bunch, but at least he had finished school. Not to mention, he had opened a successful pizza place and it was still going strong under the management of his grandson. "Let's get back on track here. What did Nigel say about the pregnancy?"

"He said. Wait. I have an audio file." After shoving the last bit of donut in her mouth, she reached in her bag, pulled out her phone, opened an app, and pressed play.

"Yes, well. That brief... *interlude* certainly disrupted Veronica's trajectory. Took her out of circulation for nearly a year, if I recall. But once the matter was 'sorted,' her father brought me in to see her restored to the academic path with *appropriate vigor*."

So we didn't *really* have any new information. Just confirmation that what Freda and Doris had said was true. Veronica *had* had a baby when she was sixteen.

Brittany paused and enjoyed the moment. Except no one was really celebrating her big discovery. "What, no applause?"

"We knew she had a baby," Antonio said. "Sorry Brittany. Freda is the baby. Doris told us."

"We don't know that Freda is the baby," Doris interjected.

Thomas tapped a dry-erase marker on the board. "We just know she *had* a baby. Remember, we are supposed to be checking Freda's facts to see if they are real."

"How can we get ahold of her birth certificate?"

"No need," Brittany said. "She posted a picture of it online to market today's episode."

Once again, she picked up her phone and opened an app. She held up the phone. A blurry picture of a birth certificate appeared.

"Let me see that," Doris commanded. Brittany handed her the phone. "Now how am I supposed to see this? It's smaller than a postage stamp." Doris pulled a pair of reading glasses out of her purse and put them on.

Brittany showed her how to enlarge the photo. Doris fiddled around with the phone, studying it this way and that.

She handed the phone back to Brittany and took her glasses off, pulled a cloth out of her dress pocket and cleaned them.

"That settles it."

"Freda is Veronica's daughter?" I asked.

"Freda is *not* Veronica's daughter."

Everyone gasped.

Thomas scribbled something on the board and then turned to ask, "How can you be sure?"

Doris set her glasses and the cloth on the table. She stood and joined Thomas at the white board. She took the marker from his hand and added a dot to Veronica's time line. "This is when the baby was born. On October 2, 2000 at 3:42 a.m. at the Steele mansion. Brittany, could you read what her birth certificate says."

"Grandview Hospital on October 2, 2000 at 9:02 a.m."

"See?" Doris handed the marker back to Thomas.

"How can you be sure of the time?" Owen asked.

"Young man. Do you have any children?" Bernice asked.

"No, I don't."

Bernice continued knitting while a tear dripped on her yarn. "When you do, you remember the exact day and time like it was yesterday."

"Oh," Owen answered. "But it wasn't her..." He pointed at Doris.

"No, son, it wasn't mine," Doris said, her voice steady but distant. "But I remember everything. That young girl wanted the baby from the moment she felt her move. I wrote the time down on the birth certificate —3:42 a.m.—and it's etched on my soul like it happened yesterday. When I handed her the baby, she clutched her close and begged her father to let her keep the baby. She screamed and cried when the adoption agency took the baby away."

The room was so silent you could hear an autumn leaf fall. Agatha broke the silence by whimpering at Emily's feet.

"She wants you to pick her up," Antonio offered.

Emily picked her up and hugged Agatha to her chest.

While everyone was still absorbing the information, Brittany stood and said, "Well, this was fun. I have a new story to write." She slung her bag over her shoulder.

James stood and smoothed his slacks. "Don't you want to know what else we find out before you go write another expose that ruins someone else's life?"

It was true he'd given Brittany permission to write about his story, but it didn't mean he wasn't suffering the repercussions. This was a turn. I was usually the one who cautioned...that's not a strong enough word...

verbally wrestled with…Brittany about posting or printing a story before checking *all* the facts.

Bernice stuffed her knitting in her bag. "This was fun, but I'm spent. Doris, Mabel, are you ready to go?"

The truth about solving mysteries is that they often cut an artery, and the pain of your past comes spewing out. I glanced at Doris—she looked deflated, saggy in a way that had nothing to do with age. Letting go of a secret she'd carried for decades—about a baby torn from a young girl's arms—had stripped her bare.

Bernice had also wiped away a tear and corrected Owen. There was a story there too, one she hadn't told yet.

Emory stood. "I'll drive you. I need to get to the morgue."

"I'll come with you," Emily said as she stood, dumping Agatha on the floor. Agatha responded with a protesting yip.

"You hurt the puppy," Antonio reached over and scooped Agatha up in his doughy arms and soothed her. "She didn't mean it," he said to Agatha.

Emily ignored the fact that she'd just let my dog fall onto the floor and fluttered her eyelashes at Emory. "Remember you promised to show me the forensic lab."

Emory responded with a goofy grin and launched into the definition of forensics. "Forensics is the scientific method of gathering and analyzing evidence from crime scenes to be used in a court of law," he began, his tone sliding into full lecture mode as the hens gathered their bags and followed him and Emily out of the room, nodding politely while he droned on about trace evidence and chemical analysis.

I sat back in my seat and wondered if anyone else was wondering how Emory had caught Emily's attention. More than that, how was he going to keep it?

"She's using him for research," James offered as if he were reading my mind. Then he glanced at Brittany, who hadn't left. "All writers do it. I just wish she was a bit more ethical about it."

Randolph spoke for the first time since the meeting had started. "You mean tell him she isn't into him?"

Antonio stroked a sleeping Agatha on his lap. "Is it bothering you?"

"Yes," James admitted. "I don't want to see Emory get hurt."

Brittany stood and paced with her arms crossed. "So you're saying she should say, 'Emory, you're kind of weird but I need to do some research on a book.'"

Randolph stood and matched her posture. "No. Emory is intelligent. Just not when it comes to relationships. She should respect him and say, 'Could you help me with some research for a book?'"

I wanted to say Brittany struggled with ethics as much as Emory struggled with relational intelligence, but that would be akin to setting off a bomb. Instead, I asked Allison, "What do you think?"

Allison straightened slightly, her posture hinting she'd been waiting for an invitation to speak. "It could work," she said with a small nod. "My husband's a real geek. I don't understand half the stuff he says about aerodynamics, but I nod along anyway."

I offered her a quick smile, but inside, I was itching to get back to the case. Not that we were making much progress. The hens had filed out. Brittany and Randolph were locked in an argument by the large calendar of upcoming Maplewood Library events. Allison probably needed to get on with her day.

I stared at the board: the baby's birth, Nigel reaching out to James when Veronica turned twenty, her birth again, and her death—nothing else. Sparse, cryptic, maddening. So far, all we really knew was that Freda had lied. Veronica wasn't her mother.

Miss Marple would say that human nature in a small town reveals itself in the smallest details—someone's raised eyebrow, a too-careful answer, a subtle slip in dates or motives. Let goosebumps be our clue. And yet, even *she* would admit that the truth can hide behind polite smiles.

The board offered no answers—only the kind of silence Miss Marple would call suspicious. One truth was clear—Freda wasn't the daughter. Which meant someone else was keeping the real secret... and they were doing a much better job of it.

CHAPTER 20
CONFESSIONS AND COFFEE CUPS

THE REST of the day at the library felt pretty normal, except for my throbbing nose and face. I didn't dare take some of the meds I'd been prescribed. They made me loopy and I'd probably say something stupid. Scratch that. I would. Not to mention, I couldn't drive home if I took them. It said that on the bottle.

I didn't think I could handle the after school program. The sad looks. The comments. Preschoolers and kindergarteners were one thing, but grade schoolers and middle schoolers were a whole different story. Not only did they tend to be louder, but their comments were also snarkier, which on a normal day, I didn't mind. But today, I felt as if my head were going to torpedo off my body and explode into a million tiny pieces.

Mary seemed to have things under control. I asked her if she could handle the after school program. She responded with, "Sure. I can handle it. I've got plenty of help today."

As I packed up my stuff and lured Agatha to the back door with a treat, my phone buzzed.

A text from Brandon.

Dinner tonight?

I texted back.

I don't feel like going out.

The three dots danced across the phone while Agatha snatched the treat from my hand and bounded back to the Children's Room.

I followed her.

"Sorry, girl. I know you're waiting on your friends." By friends, I meant the kids in the after-school program. "But I need to go home."

Mary was busy setting out snacks on the counter. She waved a cinnamon-dusted hand without looking up.

"Made pumpkin spice puppy chow. Figured they needed something sweet and seasonal before they inhaled their weight in cheddar crackers."

"Delicious and dangerous," I murmured, eyeing the sugary mix of cereal, white chocolate, and pumpkin pie spice. Agatha's nose twitched as if she agreed.

Mary bent down to scratch Agatha behind the ears. "Don't pout, sweet girl. I'll pack you a doggy bag, and you'll see all your friends again tomorrow."

My phone buzzed.

Brandon:

Then let's not go out. I'll bring soup.
And that bread you like.

Say yes, Gabby.

I stared at the screen. He remembered the rosemary focaccia. My stomach betrayed me with a growl loud enough that Agatha tilted her head.

I sighed and typed back:

Fine. But only if you bring the bread.

Three dots appeared. Followed by:

I'm already in line at the bakery.

Of course he was.

I slipped out the back door with Agatha yipping in protest as the front door chimed and the after-school program kids entered, laughing and full of energy.

I hadn't eaten lunch, I realized, as the library door closed behind me. After The Sleuths had left, I'd spent the afternoon catching up on tasks. At some point, I'd retreated to my office, finished off the rest of the donuts, and reread the email about the Grandview Library position at least ten times. Then, in a moment of poor judgment and wishful thinking, I'd browsed a Grandview real estate site full of houses I couldn't possibly afford.

I wanted to tell Brittany about the job offer. I really did. But I could see her headline now:

"Former Foster Kid Accepts Head Librarian Position At Grandview Public Library."

She'd lace the article with the traumas of my childhood, top it off with a generous dose of *I know her personally, and I've watched her rise from the gutter*, and sprinkle in her role helping me solve Councilman Bernard's murder—as well as Janet's and Ruthie's. Naturally, all the glory would go to her, the celebrated writer for *The Grandview Gazette*, for "bringing me to the city." And solving the murders, of course.

The drive home was short and the neighborhood was quiet. Good. My neighbors were still at work. Including Miranda, whom I loved but didn't want her to get wind of my promotion. Hadn't she told me she'd moved here to be a big fish in a smaller town?

I parked and went inside. For the first fifteen minutes, I changed and thought about the case.

I stood at the kitchen counter, absentmindedly stirring a mug of chamomile tea I had no intention of drinking. Agatha thumped her tail against the cabinet, watching me with her usual golden-eyed wisdom, as if she already knew the answer to the question twisting in my gut.

"Why would she lie?" I asked, though I already knew Agatha wouldn't answer. "Freda adored Veronica. She wasn't calculating. She wasn't even secretive. If anything, she was too open. She posted everything —every book review, every fan theory, every emotion."

I sank onto the stool at the island and wrapped both hands around the warm mug. "She said Veronica was her mother. Just like that. As if the truth didn't matter."

Agatha let out a soft "woof" and rested her chin on my slipper.

"She's not acting like herself," I said quietly, almost afraid to admit it out loud. "That's the part I can't shake."

I looked out the window, the maple tree swaying gently in the afternoon breeze. "As Miss Marple always said, human nature is always interesting—and people usually act the same way, over and over."

I glanced down at Agatha. "But Freda's not. She's broken her pattern. And that means something."

Agatha's tail gave a single thump, like a punctuation mark.

The question swirled around in my head like maple leaves whirling around the yard. I took some meds, and promptly fell asleep on the couch.

The doorbell chimed, rousing me from sleep.

So much for a peaceful afternoon. I stood, untangled myself from the blanket, and shuffled to the window. It was dark. I must've been out for hours. I couldn't see much, just a vague outline on the porch—tall, familiar.

I flipped on the porch light.

Brandon stood there, takeout bag in one hand, Agatha's leash in the other. She sat like a perfect angel, tail wagging, as if she knew the moment needed a touch of drama. Had I really slept through him coming in and taking Agatha out? Maybe I did need police protection.

The second I opened the door, she bounded inside, tugging the leash taut and sending Brandon stumbling forward. I stepped in, catching him as he landed against me.

He lingered there a second longer than necessary,

warm and steady, before righting himself. Without a word, he set the takeout bag on the coffee table, unclipped Agatha's leash, and turned back to me.

His gaze held mine as he stepped closer, quiet and sure, then wrapped his arms around me and murmured, "I haven't stopped thinking about that kiss at The Tasty Burger. Or you."

I didn't move. I didn't need to.

For the first time all day, I felt like I'd finally exhaled.

I didn't answer.

He continued, "I've also been thinking about the question you asked me."

I stepped back. "Which question was that?"

He chuckled and pulled me back to him and kissed me so long I forgot what day it was.

"Oh, that question."

"Oh, *that* question."

"I want to say—"

"I was offered the position of head librarian at Grandview Public Library." The words burst out before I could stop them.

He stepped back, arms dropping to his sides. "You're not going to take it, are you?"

"I... don't know." I fiddled with the sleeves of my sweater. "You know what Angela said about me."

He crossed his arms and planted his feet wide. "You're going to take a job at a big-city library because a criminal said mean things about you?"

Agatha, sensing the shift, tugged the takeout bag off the coffee table. It hit the floor with a squelch. The white paper—emblazoned with the *SOP With Soup* logo—

soaked through instantly as tomato and basil soup oozed out of the cracked container.

I lunged to grab the bag. "Agatha, not yours."

Maybe I was too sharp, but I was angry. When you get offered a big promotion, people are supposed to congratulate you—not suggest you only got it because the last librarian was a criminal.

I carried the dripping bag to the kitchen. Brandon followed behind.

He grabbed the roll of paper towels from the counter. "Can we talk about this?"

This wasn't the time to tell him there was no need. Agatha had probably already cleaned the floor better than we could.

"I think we already have," I said, voice flat.

He stood there for a moment, the paper towels in his hand, like he wasn't sure whether to stay or try again. But he didn't say anything else.

He set the roll on the counter, took a slow breath, and walked to the door.

I didn't stop him.

The door closed quietly behind him.

I peeled the lid off what remained of the soup, poured it into a bowl, and watched it drip down the side. Most of it made it. Some didn't. I grabbed a spoon and headed for the couch.

Agatha curled up beside me, letting out a low sigh like even she was tired of the tension.

I looked at the stained, sagging bag on the counter. Once white and crisp. Now wilted, red, and ruined.

It reminded me of us.

I told myself I was mad at Brandon—for hesitating,

for not being instantly supportive. But deep down, I knew the truth: I didn't believe I deserved the job either. Not really.

It was easier to see doubt in his eyes than face the constant echo in my own head: *You don't belong. You're still that girl from nowhere, trying to shelve yourself into the wrong section.*

I took a bite of soup. It was lukewarm and a little tangy.

Even if he had said all the right things, would I have believed him?

Probably not.

Not yet.

———

As I drank the last bit of soup out of the bowl, I thought about calling Brittany. The doorbell chimed, interrupting my plan.

I set the bowl down on the floor for Agatha to lick clean before peeking out the curtain. Freda. *What was she doing here?*

I dropped the curtain and went to the door. Before I could open it all the way, she tumbled in, her signature oversized purse leading the way.

"I'm here to confess." She plunked down in the armchair Bernice had been knitting in earlier today and hugged her purse.

Confess to what? *Murder?*

"How about I make us some coffee?"

She opened her purse and dug around in it before

answering. "Oh my gosh," she said to herself more than anyone. "I can't find anything in this purse."

I was regretting my argument with Brandon for more than one reason at this moment. For the I-ruined-our-relationship-forever reason and for the possibly-a-murderer-in-my-house-and-he's-the-detective reason.

She set the purse down on the floor. "Sure. I'd love a cup of coffee."

Did she have poison in that purse? Was she waiting for me to brew the coffee so she could slip it in my mug when I wasn't looking? Is that what she had done at Veronica Steele's reading at the library on Monday?

"Umm, would you like to join me in the kitchen? We can chat while I make the coffee."

"Actually, I need to use your bathroom."

I pointed down the hallway and scooped up Agatha and, much to her little doggy-dismay, I put her in the laundry room and closed the door. I didn't want my dog to be poisoned again. I'd spent an agonizing night at the vet last spring after she ingested arsenic.

I froze with indecision. Did I go in the kitchen and make the coffee, or rifle through Freda's handbag?

"I thought you were going to make coffee," Freda said as she appeared, seemingly out of nowhere.

"Sorry… the meds the doctor gave me," I pointed to my nose, "really mess with my mental capacity."

Right now my mental capacity was supercharged with suspicion. I could be in my house with a murderer and my phone was on the charger in my bedroom.

Freda blew her nose. "I can join you in the kitchen now."

Sure, she could join me in the kitchen now that she'd put the poison in her pocket.

I hadn't asked what she needed to confess to because I didn't want to know yet. Not until I called the police station. My detail out front had been removed after the Willowware teacup was a dead end. That's what small towns seemed to do when they ran into a roadblock: nothing. They didn't have the resources or the manpower to protect me, especially if they didn't know what or who to protect me from.

Their excuse was that several of the teacups from Veronica Steele's reading may have been coated. Maybe in the confusion, I'd taken one home by mistake. Lame.

I filled up the coffee maker with fresh water from the fridge before grinding beans. Freda sat at the island, sniffling and blowing her nose.

Once the coffee was brewing, I leaned up against the counter and asked, "What's going on Freda?"

"Bert and I had a fight. A big one. I don't think it is going to work out."

I grabbed the tissue box from the counter and thrust it toward her. She pulled a few more tissues from the box and blew her nose loudly.

"I just had a fight with my boyfriend, too." I shared hoping she would open up and confess.

"Really?"

The coffee maker beeped signaling the end of the brew cycle. I opened the cabinet.

"Wow, what Doris said about you is true."

I grabbed two floral mugs and set them next to the coffee maker.

"That you're like an old lady in a young body. You

collect vintage dishes…" she paused and motioned to my clothes. "You even wear retro clothes."

I thought I'd test her vintage knowledge. "Do you know anything about these?" I held up the mugs.

"Looks like something we found in my great-grandma's attic."

"Did you find any Willowware in her attic?"

"What's that?"

"The tea cups Veronica requested her tea was served in."

Her eyes grew as wide as a tea cup saucer. "Do you have any of them?"

"No…" I paused and then made a split second decision. "But Doris found one in my cabinet and it wasn't mine." I paused again for dramatic effect. "It was coated with poison."

"Oh my. That would be scary." It was her turn to pause. She jumped to her feet. "You think… I would *never*."

She circled the island like a wind-up toy cranked too tight.

Unsure of what to do, I poured the coffee into mugs and asked as she passed me, "Cream and sugar?"

That stopped her in her tracks. She put both hands on her knees and laughed. "I thought *you* were the murderer.

"I paused and then added, "Are you the murderer?"

"What?! No!" She blinked at me, then dropped onto the nearest stool like her knees had suddenly given out.

From the laundry room, Agatha started up with her yipping chorus—full-volume outrage that she wasn't invited to the excitement. I considered letting her in, but part of me needed the buffer of barking. Something to fill the space between what I'd just said and what I was starting to feel.

"Do you have raw sugar and heavy whipping cream?"

"Yes to both." I added them and used my mini frother to mix them in.

I handed over the mug. She clutched it like a lifeline, fingers tight around the ceramic.

"I didn't mean to accuse you," I said, voice softening. "It's just... the Willowware—it's not exactly common. And finding a poisoned cup tucked into my cabinet? It raises questions."

She didn't sip. Just stared at the swirl of cream. "I handed Veronica the tea cup. That's all. I swear. I wouldn't hurt Veronica—or *anyone*."

The stool creaked beneath her as she shifted, and I watched her carefully. There was fear in her eyes—but was it fear of being accused... or fear of what I might find next?

I took a calming breath and stood, heading toward the laundry room. "Let me go rescue Agatha before she brings the house down."

As I reached the door, her voice caught me mid-step. "You really thought it might've been me?"

I turned just enough to meet her gaze. "Let's just say, as Miss Marple would, it's always worth paying attention when someone stops acting like themselves."

I gave her a small smile, opened the laundry room door, and was immediately bowled over by a golden-doodle determined to get in on the mystery.

As Agatha sniffed Freda's shoes like she was verifying her alibi, I refilled my coffee and leaned against the counter. "You said you needed to confess."

"Oh yes," she said quickly, wiping her cheek. "But not to murder. Doris—Veronica's nurse—and her friends came to my hotel room. Doris said she knew I wasn't Veronica's daughter."

I took a slow sip. "Did you know?"

A tear tracked down her cheek. "Yes. I did. My parents were killed in a car accident when I was three months old. I have really great adoptive parents. They're probably going to disown me now."

I said nothing. Just waited.

"It was Bert's idea," she added, her voice brittle. "When we went to Dale's hotel room—while I was interviewing him—Bert found the will. He took photos of it. It had a clause in fine print, that if her daughter was found, she got half the estate. I... I took the manuscript."

I stood and opened the treat canister labeled **Good Dog**, handing Agatha a greenie, mostly so I'd have something to do with my hands. "I don't understand."

"When we left Dale's room," she continued, eyes fixed on a crack in the tile, "Bert said we weren't going to be left high and dry. He showed me the will, and with all the random people on it, he said if I claimed to be Veronica's daughter, we could contest it. We'd have enough money to set ourselves up for life."

"And the novel? *Twenty Years Gone*?" I asked.

"That was just a happy accident. It really fit with our plan."

I folded my arms, trying to keep my voice even. "What was your fight with Bert about?"

"I told him I was confessing everything to the police."

I raised an eyebrow. "And yet you came to my house."

She looked up, ashamed. "I thought Detective Brandon would be here."

Before I could respond, Agatha's ears perked. A half-second later, headlights swept across the living room window, then the unmistakable crunch of boots on gravel echoed up the walk.

We both turned toward the door.

Agatha let out a single, pointed yip.

I didn't move. Just stood there, coffee cooling in my hand.

Three sharp knocks rattled the back door.

CHAPTER 21
THE SUSPECTS' GATHERING

I PEERED out the small window at the top of the back door and sighed with relief. Brandon.

"Let me in, Gabby," he ordered.

I opened the door, mumbling under my breath, "Gosh, you don't have to be such a bossy pants."

Brandon stepped into the kitchen, and Agatha greeted him by launching herself into his arms like an Olympic goldendoodle gymnast. He barely acknowledged her as his glare landed on Freda, who sat at the island sipping coffee and deliberately avoiding eye contact.

"Doris called the station and said Freda was headed here."

Freda took a large gulp of her coffee and set the mug down with a definitive clink. "Because I thought you were here. Let me grab my purse. I'm ready to go."

"Go where?"

For a detective, he wasn't exactly connecting the obvious dots.

"To the police station," she said, exasperated. "I confessed everything to Gabby. But she said you two had a fight, so I figured you'd want to hear it at the station—before you booked me."

Clearly, Freda had been binging too many crime podcasts.

Brandon kept patting Agatha, but his posture shifted, shoulders tensing. I stepped a little closer, ready to catch Agatha if he dropped her to reach for handcuffs or a sidearm.

"Just to be clear," he said slowly, "you murdered Veronica?"

Freda gasped. "Of course not! What did Doris even tell you?"

"That you're not Veronica's daughter."

"I'm not," Freda admitted. "I'm guilty of lying on a podcast… and stealing a manuscript."

"And Bert took pictures of the will," I added.

Agatha, sensing the tension rising like a teakettle about to whistle, leaped from Brandon's arms and trotted toward her food bowl, clearly deciding she'd rather not be the emotional support animal in this particular moment.

Detective Brandon relaxed. "Gabby, can I speak to you in private?"

"Not yet. You need to hear what the fine print of the will says. The part that Dale neglected to tell me when we spoke."

"What does it say?"

"It says that if Veronica's daughter is found, she gets half of the estate."

Freda stood off to the side, arms crossed, tapping

her foot like a metronome on overdrive. "Can we just get this over with? I've read enough crime books to know this is where someone yells 'book her'—and then what? Do I get a phone call? Do I have to remember someone's number from memory?"

"No one is yelling 'book her,'" I said, trying to soothe her.

"I don't remember my mom's number from memory."

Brandon crossed his arms and said, "Gabby, again, can we talk privately?"

My house was small. The only private spaces were the bedroom, the guest room, and the bathroom in between them. I tried to decide which one wouldn't start the rumor mill. I mean, Freda still had a podcast. Could you podcast from jail? Would she go to jail?

Brandon grabbed my elbow and led me down the hallway to my bedroom. He shut the door behind us. Great. Let the rumor mill begin.

He faced me. "Gabby, you need to stop letting murderers in your house."

"She's not a murderer." The argument we'd had earlier still stung. I wasn't ready to let it go.

"Let me try again." He wrapped his arms around me and pulled me close. "I was worried about you."

"Aren't you worried that Freda is getting away?"

"Nope. I'm more worried about what I said earlier."

"That I got the job offer because Angela is a criminal?"

"Yes, that part."

"I think most people say congratulations when someone gets a job offer."

"Congratulations." He smiled, but it didn't quite reach his eyes. "Gabby... back in the city, I worked the Clockwork Killer case. It was brutal. He left clues like puzzles, each murder timed to the minute, like some twisted schedule. We caught him, but the cost..." He exhaled. "I didn't sleep right for months. Lost people I cared about. I told myself if I ever got out, I'd find a quiet town and build something real. Maybe even start a family."

I looked at him. He wasn't just a detective trying to keep me safe—he was someone who knew what it was to lose that safety.

"Well," I said, the edge in my voice softening. "You picked the wrong town if you were looking for peace and quiet."

"Yeah," he said, a wry smile tugging at his mouth. "But I didn't pick wrong when it came to you."

The air shifted. Slower. Warmer. Like time had curled in around us, holding its breath.

In that moment, I knew. I wasn't accepting the job. I didn't need a fresh start somewhere else. I'd already found what I was looking for. Right here. In this tiny town. In this timeworn house. With him.

I rose onto my toes and kissed him.

He didn't hesitate. His arms tightened around me like he was anchoring both of us to the one safe thing he trusted. Me.

And just like that, the world went quiet.

Not *dead* quiet. Just...full.

The door flung open and Freda stood there with Agatha.

"So that's what you needed to talk to her about? Should I do a podcast on police corruption?"

I stepped back, my face flushed. "You can take her in now."

Brandon dropped his arms. "Okay. Let's go, Freda."

With Brandon and Freda gone, the job offer declined, at least in my head, and Brandon and I back together, I could rest. Or could I? We were no closer to finding Veronica's killer, or her daughter for that matter, than we were yesterday.

I'd let Brandon take the lead on the murder case, like he'd asked, and focused on unraveling the library scandal instead. But honestly? He wasn't any closer to solving it than Brittany, The Sleuths, the hens—or me. Actually, I might've been a step ahead of all of them. Not officially, of course. But people kept confessing things to me. Not about the murder, exactly. Just…secrets. Maybe it was because, like Miss Marple, I had that unassuming, friendly face. The kind people overlooked—until they didn't.

Then it hit me. *I knew who Veronica's daughter was.* At least I had a suspicion. I needed to follow up that lead with facts. And I knew just who had those facts. I poured myself a fresh cup of coffee and sat down in my comfy chair—the same one Bernice had claimed when she was here. The coffee would most likely keep me up late. But who was I kidding? I wasn't going to sleep until I had this figured out anyway.

I thought about going to the library so I could look

at both sides of our murder board. Then I remembered what the label on my pain meds said: No driving.

I knew who the killer was, too. Freda had unknowingly handed me the final clue—one of those small, peculiar details most people overlook. But that's the thing, isn't it? The truth is always in the overlooked bits. Miss Marple would say so, and I'd learned—sometimes the hard way—to trust her.

I didn't feel triumphant. I felt... steady. Like I was standing on the last page of a mystery novel, all the pieces clicking into place, and now came the part where the amateur sleuth announces what Scotland Yard has somehow missed. But I wasn't going to confront the killer alone.

Not again.

No more shadowy corners or tense library aisles with only Agatha for backup. Last time I tried that, I ended passed out on the floor and I couldn't dial 911. I needed people. Witnesses. A place where the worst thing that usually happened was someone getting served the wrong latte.

So. The Daily Grind. Eight a.m.

A cozy coffee shop with bad acoustics and excellent lighting. Perfect for revealing secrets and identifying murderers without getting murdered yourself.

I'd invite The Sleuths, of course—they'd mutiny if I didn't. The hens too, because they'd smell gossip in the air and show up early with muffins of their own. Brittany, armed with her reporter's notebook and knack for getting the article out before an arrest. Brandon, because he needed to see what Maplewood-style sleuthing actually looked like. Scratch that. My sleuthing style. Emily. Dale. And Freda—if she wasn't still scribbling new podcast ideas from inside a holding cell.

I'd line them up in those mismatched wooden chairs like pieces on a chessboard. Not to trap anyone. Just to finally lay it all out. The timeline, the clues, the things that didn't quite fit—until they did. Until they pointed, quietly and unmistakably, to the person who thought they'd gotten away with it.

I wouldn't shout. Wouldn't accuse.

I'd do it gently. Calmly. Miss Marple-style.

Just the facts, you see. Just a librarian with a knack for murder mysteries, reminding a killer they weren't quite as clever as they thought.

I typed up a text:

> Meet me at The Daily Grind tomorrow at 8 a.m. I know who killed Veronica.

I copied and pasted it and sent it to those on my list with cell phones. I called the Airbnb where the hens were staying and spoke with Bernice, who assured me she wasn't too old to relay a phone message.

Brittany responded with a text of her own:

> I'm coming over if you don't tell me who did it now, Gabby.

I texted her back:

> See you in the morning at The Daily Grind.

I expected a text back from Brandon, but none came. He must have been busy with interviewing Freda. Finally, the confirmation from The Slueths, and a text from Emory asking:

Mind if I bring Emily?

I texted back:

I'm counting on it.

No reply from Freda, which meant she didn't have her phone in the interrogation room—or the jail cell, if Brandon had decided to keep her overnight. I hoped it was the former.

As much as I thought of Dale as a leech who didn't deserve it, I made a quick call to his hotel. Because at the end of the day, Veronica had been his wife. And I figured even Dale would want to be there when her killer was named.

Another quick phone call to Mary assured me she could handle things at the library in the morning.

I took Agatha out one last time. She did her business, and we went to bed.

I pulled the quilt up to my chin, Agatha already snoring at my feet. Tomorrow, I'd do what Miss Marple always did best—gather the suspects, follow the thread, and let the truth do the talking.

And this time, I wouldn't second-guess myself. I had the clues, the motive, the slip-up.

All I needed now was a decent night's sleep followed by a strong cup of coffee.

CHAPTER 22

KILLER AT THE DAILY GRIND

EVERYONE FILED into The Daily Grind at five til eight. First came the hens, all pastel lipstick and layered scarves, followed by James, who must have given them a ride, judging by the way Bernice was holding his arm like a prom date. Antonio, Randolph, and Thomas arrived next, already deep in debate over whether the espresso machine was truly calibrated to European standards. Brittany strolled in behind them, phone already recording.

Freda entered next, slipping in through the side door and catching my eye.

She leaned in close as the others settled, her voice low but firm. "Dale's agreed not to press charges," she said. "As long as I return the manuscript, take down the podcast episode, and publicly retract the daughter claim on social media."

I nodded. That was better than a courtroom circus.

Then Emory arrived, Emily on his arm. She wore a cream blouse and a look of serene innocence that didn't fool me one bit. I scanned the room, then turned to Doris, who stood by the register pretending not to listen.

"Now?" I asked quietly.

Doris gave a small nod. "The date and time on her birth certificate match. Plus, that small heart-shaped birthmark on her neck was there the day she was born."

That was all I needed.

I stood and cleared my throat. Everyone hushed. Even Agatha stopped snuffling under the table.

"Thank you all for coming," I began, trying to steady my voice. "I believe I now know who killed Veronica Steele. But before we get there, a few things need saying."

I turned to Emily. "You knew Veronica was your mother. You found out while she was mentoring you."

Emily's face paled, but she lifted her chin. "She told me during one of our coaching sessions. At first, she wanted to get to know me. She was kind, even maternal. But something changed. She became...moody. She told me to never tell anyone. Said it would ruin her. Then she stole my manuscript."

This all fit with what Emory had texted me about brain tumors earlier in the case—mood swings, paranoid behavior.

Since Dale already knew, I dropped the next bomb to see how Emily would react. I pulled out my phone and read Emory's text about the post-mortem:

> Veronica had a brain tumor. Frontal lobe. Big one. Glioblastoma...She wouldn't have made it six months

There were murmurs around the room.

"I knew… I mean …" She paused and smoothed out her jeans. "Emory told me."

Randolph and Detective Brandon stood at the same time. Randolph beat Brandon to the punch by saying, "Emory, I don't care how smitten you are—sharing autopsy details without confirming next-of-kin? That's reckless. You crossed a line, and you know it."

Brandon opened his mouth to say something, then closed it, gave Randolph a quick nod, and sat back down.

I gave the crowd a moment to absorb the she-was-already-dying bombshell, watching their faces closely. Emily and Emory both fidgeted, suddenly fascinated by the floor instead of each other.

"You're right, Randolph. I shouldn't have told her. But she's Veronica's daughter. Don't you think she had a right to know?"

"Of course she did," Doris interjected. "But not before Veronica's murderer is behind bars." Then she gasped, hand flying to her mouth.

"Does someone need to spell it out for you, Doris?"

"Someone needs to spell it out for me," Mabel chimed in.

"What are we spelling? I thought this was a whodunit meeting," Antonio muttered, dragging a beefy hand over his face.

Bernice continued knitting, and for a moment I felt like I'd stepped straight into a Miss Marple mystery. With the silver curls glowing beneath the trendy overhead lights and her needles clicking in perfect rhythm, Bernice transformed. She swayed gently, casting the kind of stillness that demands attention. When the room went quiet—just the steady clack of her knitting—she spoke.

"Emily murdered her mother. If she'd known Veronica was already dying, she would've waited it out."

Emory, who had been casually resting his bony arm across Emily's shoulders since the floor-staring began, dropped it like it had caught fire at the autumn harvest bonfire.

Emily buried her face in her hands. "I didn't…"

"So you came to the reading to confront her?" I asked.

"I did. But I didn't have the nerve. Not really. I just wanted to shake her a little. Embarrass her. I slipped something into her drink—nothing fatal. Just enough to make her seem drunk."

Antonio muttered, "So the sweet-faced one did it. Always the quiet ones."

Emory rose beside her, placing a hand on her shoulder. "You remember what the toxicology report said, Emily?" He turned to face me. "She didn't kill her."

Brandon and I spoke at the same time. "You knew Emily poisoned her?"

Emory's chair scraped back as he stood, indignant. "Excuse me? Emily didn't murder anyone." His voice cracked with restrained fury. "Not to mention Veronica stole Emily's manuscript and was publishing it as her own."

"You mean *Twenty Years Gone* is your book, Emily?" Freda chimed in, her voice teetering between disbelief and awe.

Huge tears streamed down Emily's pale cheeks. "Yes," she whispered, voice shaking. "It was a message to my mother. Obviously, she didn't get the message."

A hush fell over the room, broken only by the soft hum of the cafe lights. Even Agatha stilled, ears pricked. James shifted uncomfortably. Randolph blinked hard, like he wasn't quite sure where to look.

Owen, ever the opportunist, cleared his throat. "That explains the tone. And the details. But it doesn't change what I found," he said, tapping the worn edge of his notebook.

The room shifted. Chairs creaked. Antonio let out a low whistle.

Owen continued, "I've contacted five other authors," he said. "All missing manuscripts. All had worked with Veronica. So that part of James's story, and Emily's, tracks."

Randolph looked stunned. James let out a breath like he'd been holding it for a week. Brittany angled her phone for better audio.

Agatha licked frosting from under a nearby chair.

That's when Dale brushed past my table. He bumped it just slightly—enough to send my napkin fluttering and my gaze downward to Agatha, who gave a low, rumbling growl. I didn't see him drop anything in my cup. But after two sips of my espresso, something was wrong.

My vision blurred. My tongue felt thick. The room tilted.

I caught Dale's gaze as he sat down across the room, his mouth twitching into a grin that didn't reach his eyes. Like a dog who finally caught the squirrel.

I stood—or tried to. My voice came out too loud, too slurred. "It was you."

Everyone turned.

"You broke into my house," I said, the words sticking like honey. "You put the Willowware tea cup there to poison me. And you poisoned Veronica too."

Gasps. Chairs scraped. Emily collapsed in Emory's arms.

Then everything tilted sideways, and I dropped with it.

Blackness rushed up to meet me.

Agatha barked once, sharply, as if to say "told you so."

———

When I awoke, I was tucked tightly into crisp white sheets that smelled like antiseptic.

"Gabby, you're awake," Brittany said, her chestnut waves grazing my forehead as she leaned in to plant a quick kiss there. "You have to stop putting yourself into dangerous situations."

My mouth felt as if it were stuffed full of cotton balls. I opened my mouth to speak but nothing came out. Dangerous situations? We were in a crowded coffee shop with a detective present—*my* detective.

"I'm calling Detective Brandon." She turned toward the window overlooking the parking lot. "Gabby's awake… no I haven't talked to the doctor yet… Emily is next door… I'll go check on her."

While Brittany talked, I managed to pour myself a glass of water and swish some around in my mouth.

When she finished her call with Brandon, I asked, "Did Dale confess?"

"Are you kidding me? When you and Emily both…"

"Wait, he poisoned Emily too?"

She grabbed the olive green faux leather recliner, and scooted it closer to the hospital bed. "Oh, before I forget. My mom sent over some pumpkin chocolate chip muffins." She fished in her bag and pulled out a glass container, opened it, and handed me one.

"So yeah, you and Emily passed out at the same time. At first, I thought she was like one of those fragile women who passes out from shock, like in those mystery books."

"You mean like me?"

"I wasn't going to say that." She shifted in her seat and continued. "So I called 911 and Brandon picked you up off the floor where you'd fallen. Agatha was licking your face trying to get you to wake up."

"Dale bumped my table and Agatha growled. I should have known something was up."

Brittany pulled another muffin out of the glass container and peeled the muffin liner off. "Because he bumped your table?" She shoved the muffin in her mouth and took a large bite.

"No. Because Agatha growled. While I was looking under the table at her, he slipped the poison in my cup."

She chewed thoughtfully for a moment. "So he did the same to Emily?"

I grabbed a second muffin before gulping some water. My brain fog was lifting, and the picture I'd gotten so horribly wrong was becoming clearer. "Yes.

He didn't want to lose his leech-like lifestyle and give the money to Emily. He added poison to Veronica's tea at the reading. So she was drugged by Emily but the poison Dale added killed her."

"Owen says the other people listed in Veronica's will were probably authors she plagiarized. In her brain tumor-driven mania, she was trying to make it right."

Brittany stood, dusted some crumbs off her jeans and explained, "I told Brandon I'd check on Emily. He still has to question her."

"I'm coming," I stated matter-of-factly.

"Can you walk?"

I swung my legs over the side of the bed, stood, wobbled, and sat down hard on the edge of the bed.

"I'll go find a wheel chair," Brittany offered.

In less than thirty seconds, she was back with a wheelchair and Bella, the nurse I went to high school with who had a crush on Detective Brandon.

Bella wore lilac scrubs and, with both hands on her hips, said, "I told Brittany the patient should stay in bed."

Brittany wheeled the wheelchair over to the bed despite Bella's protests. I slid into it.

"The patient's name is Gabby," I said.

"And the patient is simply being wheeled next door to check on another patient," Brittany added as she wheeled me out of the room.

Emily was sitting up in bed sipping on ice water. Her skin was the color of parchment paper.

Brittany wheeled me beside the bed and asked, "How are you?"

"Am I going to jail for murder?"

It was then that it occurred to me that Emily knew nothing. She didn't even know Dale had poisoned her. So Brittany and I filled her in, including the part about Dale marrying Veronica for her money and his consternation to her draining their accounts.

Brittany offered her a pumpkin muffin, which I'd grabbed at the last minute and carried over on my lap.

"He is the one who added the lethal dose of poison to Veronica's tea at the reading."

"So I'm not going to prison for life, just for drugging my mother."

I ignored her statement because I didn't know what she would be charged with. I plowed on with another detail. "Dale broke into my house and put a teacup laced with poison in my cupboard."

"She didn't drink out of it because Doris found it first," Brittany explained.

I would have found it because I know all my teacups, but this wasn't the time to say that.

Our conversation was cut short when Emory arrived, breathless. He entered the room in a tangle of elbows and urgency, clutching a modest bouquet of pale purple flowers.

"I've been being questioned at the police station, or I would've been here sooner." He gulped, his Adam's apple bouncing like a yo-yo. "I brought you *Echinacea purpurea*. Purple coneflowers."

He glanced down at the bouquet like it might explain him better than his words could. "They're used to modulate immune response—reduce inflammation, even lower cortisol and cytokines like IL-6. Thought they might help with...you know." He made a vague circling motion near his own chest. "Stress."

A pause. Then, more quietly, "And they're...resilient. Like you."

This was the moment I had been waiting for. Time to discover whether Emily was using Emory for his information about the case, or to write her latest book, or if she really liked him.

"Thank you, Emory. That's so sweet of you."

Emily sniffed once, then twice, her fingers tightening around the stems of the bouquet. She looked up at Emory, cheeks flushed.

"Thank you, Emory. That's...really thoughtful." She paused, glancing down at the petals, twisting the stem in her hand. "I—I actually read recently that *Echinacea purpurea* has been shown—well, in some studies—to cut the risk of respiratory infections by nearly half in people with weakened defenses." She caught herself, clearing her throat. "And lower inflammation. And maybe help balance stress hormones, too."

Her eyes flicked back to Emory, with a shy smile. "So... I guess, if the flowers help in more ways than one, that's kind of...nice." She tucked a loose curl behind her ear. "I'm not exactly graceful at saying these things."

Second major thing I got wrong today. Okay. Going back to my room and climbing into bed. I waved at Brittany to capture her attention. I nodded my head toward the door and she wheeled me out as Emory and Emily continued to whisper sweet scientific nothings to each other.

Brittany left me to take out Agatha, who'd been

deposited at my house earlier, clearly not thrilled to be left behind while her person was in the hospital.

I fell asleep until a second forehead kiss awakened me.

I swallowed and tried to clear my cotton-ball mouth. "Brittany?"

"No. It's me, Brandon, your fiancé."

CHAPTER 23
HAPPILY EVER AFTER...
WITH CAKE

MONDAY NIGHT FOUND me at Book Club once again. It seemed as if the whole town was in attendance. The one thing not in attendance—the anxious pressure felt the week before when Veronica Steele, guest speaker and murder victim, made demands no one could keep.

There was no guest speaker tonight, maybe never again. Tonight's goal was to pick our next read and give the hens a proper send off.

"This was the most exciting trip of my year," Bernice said as she entered the library talking, with her knitting back slung over her shoulder. "But I'll be honest ladies, no more murders."

"Or attempted murder," Doris added, bending to pat Agatha, who had greeted them at the door, no doubt hoping to score a donut.

Mabel brought up the rear. "Bernice, you should enjoy tonight. It may be your last vacation because you know you are—"

"Eighty-five," Bernice finished for her. "After this week, I'm feeling younger than ever." She swung her knitting bag around, nearly braining Mabel who ducked just in time.

There were not going to be any donuts at tonight's meeting. I'd ordered a cake to celebrate. Antonio and Thomas promised to pick it up on the way over.

James and Owen walked in together. Good—they'd made up. I'd been worried the whole *Veronica stole your manuscript* debacle might keep James from mentoring other authors, not to mention wreck his friendship with Owen—especially now that Owen's book was climbing the crime fiction bestseller list. James's broad back blocked my view of Emily trailing behind them, head down, moving with hesitant steps. I guessed that meant she was out of jail. For now.

Freda zipped in behind them, her oversized headphones looped around her neck and a pink microphone in hand. She wore a sweatshirt that read "Murder, She Podcasted" in bold bubble letters.

"Big news!" she said, skidding to a stop beside me with the energy of someone who drank their coffee iced with a triple-shot. "I'm launching *Whodunit Weekly*—a podcast for and about crime fiction writers. Interviews, plot twists, spicy reader questions. It's going to be Maplewood's most thrilling audio experience."

"That sounds amazing," I said, genuinely impressed. "Are you recording in a studio?"

She scoffed. "Please. The library's got better acoustics—and better coffee. If that's okay with you."

"Of course."

She held up her clipboard like a press pass. "I want

Owen as my first guest. His book is climbing the charts and, let's face it, he's got that tortured-genius thing going."

She marched over to where Owen was quietly testing coffee temperature like a chemist, and plopped down beside him. "Hey, bestselling author. Free Monday at noon?"

Owen blinked, the look on his face halfway between confusion and hatching an escape plan. "For… what?"

"For *Whodunit Weekly*," she said, already pulling out a second mic. "You, me, a conversation about crime, character arcs, and how you plan to spend your fame. You in?"

I went into the fishbowl room and started a fresh pot of coffee. I'd already brewed one pot and it was ready in a carafe, but with the crowd of Maplewood traipsing in, we'd need more. No tea though. I'd had my fill of tea. I'd also decided that to be on the safe side, I'd monitor the drinks and keep a lid on my coffee mug so no one could slip anything in mine.

Dale was going to jail for life, but I still didn't feel completely at ease. Sure, I didn't have the pressure of trying to keep a celebrity author happy, but the after effects of being poisoned in public were still raw and fresh.

Brandon's voice rang clear and strong as he greeted the hens. I peeked in the chrome of the coffee machine, tucking my copper hair behind my ears. The swelling on my face had gone down and with the expert touch of Miranda's makeover powers, I looked like I had a large nose, not a purple blob.

"Let me help you," Miranda said as she peeked in the door of the fishbowl room.

"Thanks." I handed her a tray of mugs to take out.

"I'm so glad you invited me to book club last spring." She took the tray and turned at the last minute. "You were right. This is the most exciting place in town. Murders. Mayhem. And enough gossip to keep my realtor office happy all year."

I don't remember saying *that*. But whatever. I noticed she'd brought a few of her coworkers, who both waved at me through the glass.

I smoothed my hair one more time before going out to find Brandon. I picked up the carafe and followed Miranda out, greeting her coworkers and others on the way.

"I'm here with the cake," Antonio announced as he stepped in the main door with a bakery box.

"I'm sorry, Gabby," Thomas said as he removed his plaid scarf. "I tried to stop him."

"Stop him from what?"

Antonio waddled over to the table housing the mugs Miranda had just set down. I joined him at the table and set the carafe down as he opened the box. I put a hand to my mouth and gasped.

Thomas sidled up next to me and stared at the cake with me. "From that."

Instead of saying "goodbye" or "we'll miss you Grandview crew," it read "Happy Engagement, Brandon and Gabby."

Antonio chuckled and his dough-like belly shook like he was Santa. "I did good, right?'

I had no words. What should I do? Run back to my

office and hide for the rest of the evening? James could lead book club, right?

Allison sidled up to me. "Ohhh, I want to see the cake." Agatha rested in her arms, the look of a dog who'd just eaten more treats than doggedly possible.

I slammed the lid down. "In a bit."

"It's a surprise," Antonio explained, moving his bulk in front of the box. He reached over and grabbed a mug and shoved it at her. "Have some coffee."

Allison continued to pat Agatha, who rested comfortably in the crook of her arm. "I hope you don't mind. I fed her a few doggy treats that Ned insisted I bring her."

"I don't mind at all." I stifled a nervous laugh and patted the bakery box. "Better than cake."

Maybe I could bring the meeting to order and take the attention off the bakery box.

A large rap followed by Thomas's signature former councilman voice said, "Let's bring this meeting to order." He winked at me and continued. "Find a seat."

Feet shuffled. Chairs creaked. Everyone found a seat and looked at him with rapt attention.

He stood straight, gripping the cafe-style table like a podium, one hand on each side. After clearing his throat, he spoke with the measured authority of a public official addressing a press conference. "Let me begin by saying we are deeply saddened by the loss of Veronica Steele. We are also relieved that the perpetrator is now in custody and that our head librarian is safe."

Brittany appeared as if out of nowhere and joined him. "Brittany Lawson is going to give us a brief update. Please keep your questions until the end."

He was totally rocking the press-conference vibe.

"Thank you, Thomas." He stepped back and she dumped her leather satchel on the cafe table and leaned her elbows on it. "Dale, Veronica's husband, is in jail for her murder. Emily…are you here?" She scanned the crowd. "There you are. Come up here."

Emily moved from her chair with the speed of a sloth until Doris rose and took her by the elbow, guiding her to Brittany.

"This is Emily, Veronica Steele's daughter," Doris stated and went back to her seat.

"Thank you, Doris. Emily has decided to stay in Maplewood for a while."

I think that was code for "until her trial for drugging her mother." I was proud of Brittany for not putting a negative spin on Emily's story.

Emory, who I hadn't seen come in, marched up in a disjointed fashion, put his arm around Emily, and said, "I'm helping her with research."

"I bet you are," Bernice called out.

"Bernice," Mabel chided.

"What. I know I'm old. But I'm not dead."

Thomas stood and cleared his throat.

"That's all folks. James is going to lead the discussion on our next read."

James strode to the podium, but before he could get there, Antonio jogged up and yelled, "I have an announcement."

Brandon was sitting in the front row grinning.

"This is an engagement party for Gabby and Brandon. I brought a cake!"

I turned twenty shades of red maple leaf and froze.

Brandon stood and added, "Everyone have some cake."

As chairs scraped and folks began lining up for slices of the unexpected engagement cake, I stood frozen—half horrified, half amused.

"Don't just stand there," Brittany whispered, nudging me. "At least pretend to be engaged."

Brandon sidled up next to me and whispered, "We can call it a soft launch?"

Agatha barked approvingly from someone's lap, licking frosting off her snout like she'd known all along.

I looked around at the town that never minded their own business, the cake that said way too much, and the man smiling beside me.

"Only in Maplewood," I muttered.

And then I did the most unexpected thing of all.

I laughed.

———

What to read next: *Winter Wedding Murder: A Cozy Maplewood Mystery of Past Crimes, Wedding Chaos, and One Clever Goldendoodle*

NOTES

8. WRESTLE MANIA AT THE TASTY BURGER

1. Agatha Christie, *The Mirror Crack'd from Side to Side*

ABOUT THE AUTHOR

Kathleen Guire is the mother of seven, four through adoption, NiNi of fifteen, former National Parent of the Year, author, teacher, and speaker. She loves connecting with readers through her website (Kathleenguireau thor.com).

For more information,
about Kathleen, check out her website and follow her
on social media!
www.kathleenguireauthor.com
kathleenguire@gmail.com
https://linktr.ee/kguire

KATHLEEN GUIRE'S OTHER COZY MYSTERIES

COZY CORNER MYSTERIES

Fatal Fixer-Upper: A Christian Cozy Mystery of Murder, Suspense, and Reality TV

Crimecaster Cold Case: A Christian Cozy Mystery in the Pursuit of a Serial Killer

Winter Camping Caper: A Cozy Mystery of Murder, Secrets, and Survival in the Snow

MAPLEWOOD MYSTERIES

Dead Quiet At The Library

Book Club Murder: A Bookish Sleuth And Mystery Straight Out of an Agatha Christie Novel